LEGACY OF A SOLDIER

BEYOND THE UNIFORM - 1

ADITI RAY

Dedicated to the brave souls who fought in Kargil and every battle that came before and after it. To the families who lost their loved ones, who never returned home as heroes, but will forever be our heroes. To those whose names remain unknown, their sacrifices uncelebrated, yet their courage unmatchable. To the fallen warriors who endured it all, their hearts burning with devotion to their motherland. To every spirit that lives on in the hearts of those who remember. Your sacrifices echo through time, and you will never be forgotten.

Contents

Preface

This book is a work of fiction. The names, characters, and events described are entirely products of my imagination. While the backdrop of the story is set during the Kargil conflict, the details of conversations, relationships, and the unfolding events are not based on real accounts. The descriptions are inspired by what I have read, heard, and learned about the war, but they remain a blend of interpretation and imagination.

The Kargil conflict was a defining moment in our history, a time when bravery and sacrifice became the cornerstones of our nation's collective memory. This story is not an attempt to recount the events as they happened but to create a narrative that reflects the spirit of those who lived through the unimaginable. It is my way of paying tribute to the soldiers who fought not just with weapons, but with their hearts, their determination, and their unyielding love for their country.

I was moved to write this story because the life of a soldier is one of paradoxes: courage and vulnerability, discipline and chaos, loyalty and longing. The protagonist of this book represents all those who left behind the comfort of home and family, stepping into the harsh unknown with nothing but faith and duty to guide him. Through his journey, I wanted to explore the emotional and psychological toll of war—the camaraderie that becomes a lifeline, the quiet moments of reflection amidst the chaos, and the resilience that emerges from sheer necessity.

As I wrote, I found myself imagining the stories of countless soldiers whose voices may never be heard and may remain unsung. This story is for them. It is also for those who wait at home—the families, the loved ones—who carry a different kind of burden, living each day in hope and fear.

This book is my way of connecting with that enduring spirit of humanity, courage, and sacrifice. It is not meant to glorify war but to offer a glimpse into the hearts of those who endure it, reminding us of their sacrifices and the peace they strive to protect.

I wanted to mention that Hindi dialogues have been included to preserve the authenticity and cultural flavour of the narrative. To assist with understanding, footnotes have been provided for translations. I hope this doesn't disrupt the flow of your reading experience. As writers, we sometimes have to make difficult choices to balance storytelling with accessibility, and I appreciate your patience with this approach.

I hope this story resonates with you, as it did with me while writing it.

- Aditi Ray

Prologue

The summer sun dipped low over Bhairavgarh, casting golden hues over the sprawling fields that had sustained the Rathore family. Lieutenant Arjun Rathore stood before the weathered stone house that had once been his sanctuary. The ancestral home, now silent, bore the weight of memories—of laughter, struggle, and love. This would be his final visit before reporting for Operation Vijay. He had come back to pay his respects to his parents, Mahavir and Radha, whose absence echoed in every corner of the house. Their simple lives as farmers had shaped him, instilling in him the values of hard work and integrity. Now, as he prepared to leave for war, he felt a deep need to seek their silent blessing.

Arjun knelt before the small shrine in the courtyard, lighting a diya in their memory. The flickering flame seemed to dance with the wind, as though his parents were there, watching over him. He whispered, his voice thick with emotion, "Give me the strength to do my duty."

The journey that had brought him here—both to this house and this moment—had begun decades earlier.

CHAPTER ONE

DUTY CALLS

Mahavir Rathore was a man of quiet dignity, the kind of person whose presence commanded respect without the need for words. Born and raised in the small village of Bhairavgarh, near Tonk, a town near Jaipur, he had inherited his father's small yet fertile fields. Unlike the tales of despair often associated with farmers in India, Mahavir's life was a testament to resilience and hard work. His fields, meticulously maintained, yielded enough to provide a stable life for his family. He was not wealthy by any means, but he had managed to carve out a life of modest comfort, where no one in his household ever went to bed hungry.

The Rathore home was a simple yet sturdy structure, built decades ago with the help of Radha's uncle. Radha, Mahavir's wife, had lost her parents at a young age. Orphaned and vulnerable, she had been taken in by her uncle, Subedar Ramnath Singh, a retired officer in the Indian Army. Ramnath was a stern but kind-hearted man who had raised Radha as his own daughter. It was he who had ensured that she learned the values of discipline, compassion, and resilience—qualities that later shaped her as a wife and mother.

When Radha married Mahavir, Ramnath had offered his savings and his labour to help build their home. The house stood as a testament to his love and dedication. Its walls, made of stone and mud, were a pale beige from the clay that held them together. The roof was a patchwork of terracotta tiles, carefully placed to keep out the monsoon rains. A small veranda ran along the front, shaded by a neem tree that Ramnath himself had planted when the house was completed.

Though Subedar Ramnath Singh had passed away a few years after the house was built, due to old age, his presence was still felt in every corner of the house. The neem tree, with its broad, leafy branches, provided more than just shade. It was a living reminder of the man who had been a pillar of strength for Radha during her formative years. On many evenings, Radha would sit under the tree, lost in thought, her hands busy peeling vegetables while her heart replayed memories of her uncle's stories about Army life and the values of courage and sacrifice.

Inside, the house was humble but well-kept. Wooden beams stretched across the ceiling, and the floors were made of cool, polished cement. Radha's touch was evident in the neat arrangement of everything, from the clay pots in the kitchen to the faded but clean curtains that swayed gently with the breeze. Despite its simplicity, the home radiated warmth—a sanctuary built on love, sacrifice, and hard work.

Radha was the heart of the household. A woman of unparalleled strength and compassion, she complemented Mahavir's quiet demeanour with her warmth and vitality. She had a knack for turning the simplest ingredients into delicious meals, filling the house with the aroma of freshly baked rotis and fragrant curries. Her hands were often smeared with flour, yet she always found time to run them through Arjun's hair, teasing him about his wild dreams and untamed energy.

Her life had not been easy, but she had never allowed hardship to break her spirit. Losing her parents at a young age and then her beloved uncle later in life could have left her bitter. Instead, she chose to channel her grief into nurturing her family. The discipline and resilience instilled in her by her uncle were evident in the way she managed the household, cared for her son, and supported her husband.

Mahavir, on the other hand, was a man of few words. His dreams were simple but deeply rooted. He wanted to give Arjun an education that would open doors to a life beyond the confines of Bhairavgarh. Mahavir had never ventured far from the village himself, his world defined by the rhythms of farming. But he had seen enough to know that education was a key that could unlock opportunities. He wanted Arjun to have choices and to live a life where he could dream without limitations.

The Rathores were not wealthy, but they lived with a quiet sense of pride and contentment. Mahavir and Radha had worked tirelessly to create an environment where their son could flourish. They had no idea that Arjun's path would take him far beyond their wildest imaginations.

From a young age, Arjun showed a spark that set him apart. He was curious, restless, and full of questions. While other children in the village were content playing in the fields, Arjun was often found perched on the neem tree, staring at the horizon as if searching for something beyond the visible world. Mahavir would watch his son's antics with a mix of amusement and concern. He didn't fully understand the boy's restless spirit, but he knew it was a sign of something special.

Despite his reserved nature, Mahavir was a father who led by example. He never spoke about his struggles openly, but his actions were a lesson in perseverance and integrity. On many mornings, Arjun would wake up to find his father already in the fields. Mahavir's hands were calloused from years of tilling the soil, but his heart was soft, especially when it came to his family.

The village often whispered about Mahavir's insistence on sending Arjun to the best school in the district.

"Why spend so much on education when the boy will just end up in the fields?" some neighbours would say.

Mahavir ignored them. He believed in his son's potential, even if he couldn't articulate it. For Mahavir, education was not just about books; it was about giving Arjun the tools to build a future of his choosing.

As Arjun grew older, his dreams began to take shape. Inspired by the tales of bravery of his great-uncle that his mother told him at bedtime and those that he overheard in the market, he started imagining a life of adventure and purpose. Little did he know that the values he absorbed from both his parents and the legacy of his great-uncle h would one day guide him in ways even they could not have foreseen.

When Arjun was ten, an event in the village market became the catalyst for his destiny. It was an ordinary day until a group of goons stormed in, targeting a poor farmer over a false debt. The man's cries for help went unanswered as the crowd watched in fearful silence. Just when it seemed all hope was lost, a figure emerged from the crowd—a man in the olive-green uniform of the Indian Army.

The soldier's presence was commanding. Without raising his voice, he confronted the goons, his calmness masking the storm that lay beneath. One of the goons lunged at him, but the soldier dodged effortlessly, subduing him with a swift, precise move. The rest fled, their bravado crushed. The crowd erupted in cheers, but young Arjun was spellbound. The soldier's valour and composure left an indelible mark on him.

Later that evening, Arjun couldn't contain his excitement.

"Who kaun tha?"[1] he asked his father, his eyes wide with wonder.

Mahavir's face softened with admiration. "Army officer, beta." he said. "Humarein desh ka rakshak."[2]

From that day onward, Arjun's life took a new direction. He began to exhibit a sense of bravery and justice well beyond his years. When bullies at school picked on younger children, Arjun stood firm, shielding them with unwavering determination. In one instance, when a classmate was being harassed for losing a borrowed book, Arjun intervened, offering his own pocket money to replace it.

"Tum hamesha doosron ki madad karte ho,"[3] his teacher once said. "Yeh ek bahut acha un hai, Arjun. Isse banaye rakhna."[4]

Arjun's courage extended to the playground as well. During a village cricket match, a dispute broke out between two teams, threatening to escalate into a full-blown fight. While others stood by nervously, Arjun stepped in, mediating with a maturity that astonished the elders. His composed yet firm approach diffused the situation, earning him respect from players and onlookers alike.

But the most significant act of bravery came during the monsoon season, when the rains lashed against the earth, making the River Banas swell and rage with an unpredictable fury. A group of children, unaware of the dangers, had ventured too close to the riverbank. Their carefree laughter echoed through the air, as they splashed about near the water's edge, oblivious to the growing strength of the current beneath the surface.

Suddenly, in a heartbeat, the current seized one of the children, a young boy named Dev, and pulled him into its churning depths. The sound of his startled cry cut through the air, sending a ripple of panic through the group. Their laughter turned to screams, and the other children scrambled back, but Dev was already being swept away, flailing helplessly against the unforgiving waters.

Arjun, who had been sitting nearby, saw the danger unfold before him in a flash. His heart raced, not with fear, but with instinct. Without a second thought, he surged to his feet and dashed toward the river. The others stood frozen, too terrified to act, but Arjun was already in motion, diving headfirst into the violent waters. The cold shock of the river hit him like a wall, but he didn't hesitate. His focus was solely on the boy's desperate cries, which were now growing faint as the current dragged him further downstream.

The water pulled at him relentlessly, but Arjun fought against it with all his strength. He swam as though the very life of the child depended on it—because it did. The waves crashed against him, nearly knocking the wind out of him, but he pressed on, each stroke bringing him closer to Dev. As the boy's face appeared above the surface for a fleeting moment, Arjun stretched out his hand and grabbed him, pulling him close. The current fought back, but Arjun held on with fierce determination, using every ounce of his energy to drag the boy back to safety.

Finally, after what felt like an eternity, Arjun managed to get Dev to the riverbank. Exhausted and drenched, he collapsed onto the muddy ground, his chest heaving as he gasped for air. Dev, coughing and trembling, was in his arms, but he was alive. His wide, frightened eyes met Arjun's, filled with a mixture of fear and gratitude.

The child's parents, who had been watching in horror from a distance, rushed forward, their faces pale with worry. When they saw their son in one piece, their relief was palpable. The mother, her hands shaking, knelt beside Dev, pulling him into a tight embrace, tears streaming down her face.

The father, equally overcome with emotion, turned to Arjun. His voice cracked as he spoke, "Beta...Tumne aaj humein bacha liya."[5]

Arjun, still soaked to the bone, simply nodded, too overwhelmed to speak. His body trembled from the cold, but knowing that he had saved a life filled him with something far more powerful. He had acted without thinking, and now the true weight of his actions began to sink in.

Though he didn't feel like a hero, he had simply done what needed to be done, but to the family, and the village, he was more than just a boy who had saved another. He was a symbol of courage, a reminder that sometimes, in the face of fear and uncertainty, bravery can make all the difference.

Through these incidents, Arjun's resolve to become a soldier only grew stronger. He devoured every movie about war and Indian soldiers, his heart swelling with pride at their sacrifices. Each reel reinforced his vision of standing tall in the olive-green uniform, protecting his nation.

Mahavir noticed his son's growing fascination but attributed it to childish curiosity. His only goal was to ensure Arjun received a good education. Despite limited resources, Mahavir managed to enrol him in the best school in the district. Arjun excelled, his discipline and determination setting him apart. When he graduated from high school, Mahavir made another bold decision: to send Arjun to college in Delhi.

The day Arjun left for Delhi was etched in his memory. Mahavir handed him a worn-out suitcase and a small bundle of money. "Yeh hi tera mauka hai, beta,"[6] he said, his voice steady despite the emotion in his eyes. "Humein garv mehsoos karwa."[7]

Arjun could feel his father's pride, but there was an unspoken weight in Mahavir's expression—a quiet worry that his son was stepping into the world on his own. Mahavir had always been a man of few words, yet in that moment, his eyes spoke volumes. The love, hope, and silent concern were all there. His father, the rock of their family, had never shown vulnerability. But today, as he handed over the money, Arjun noticed the faintest shimmer of tears that threatened to escape.

While Mahavir's emotions were evident, Radha's face was composed, a picture of strength and serenity. She stood tall, her posture unwavering, as if she had already faced a thousand storms. Radha had always been the silent warrior of their home, the one who held everything together, even when life seemed to challenge them at every turn. Arjun had often wondered how she did it—how she could remain so calm, no matter what came their way.

As Arjun knelt to touch his mother's feet, Radha placed her hands on his shoulders, lifting him up with gentle strength. Her gaze met his, and in that moment, time seemed to stand still. There was no need for words. Her eyes conveyed a lifetime of resilience and faith, the kind that only someone who had braved many battles could possess.

"Tum achha karoge, Arjun,"[8] she said softly, her voice steady yet warm. "Lekin yaad rakhna, shakti andar se aati hai. Duniya tumhari pariksha legi, par kabhi mat bhoolna ki tum kaun ho."[9]

Arjun admired his mother for her unwavering courage. She had faced hardships with a grace that seemed almost otherworldly. It was as if she had already been through some kind of training—an emotional Army training for the soul. Whether it was financial struggles or the loss of loved ones, Radha had always stayed strong, never once letting her emotions overwhelm her. She had been their family's rock, ensuring there was always light, even on the darkest days.

As Arjun stood there, absorbing his mother's words, he noticed a subtle shift in her expression. Beneath her calm exterior, there was a quiet sadness in her eyes. It wasn't the sadness of missing her child—it was the sadness of a mother who knew the time had come for her son to face the world on his own.

Mahavir, watching the exchange silently, cleared his throat. The faintest trace of tears had escaped his eyes, but he quickly wiped them away. "Apna khayal rakhna, Arjun. Aur yaad rakhna, chahe tum kahin bhi jao, hum hamesha tumhare saath hain."[10]

Radha placed a hand on Mahavir's shoulder, offering him silent comfort. She had always been the one to ground him, to reassure him in times of uncertainty.

As Arjun turned to leave, a mixture of excitement and fear surged within him. Delhi was a city of endless possibilities, but also of unknowns. Would he live up to his parents' expectations? Would he have the strength to face the challenges ahead?

As he boarded the bus, he glanced out the window and saw his parents standing side by side, watching him leave. Mahavir stood tall, his eyes filled with pride, while Radha remained stoic, her look steady and unwavering. Arjun knew that, no matter what, he carried the strength of both his mother and father within him.

The bus ride from Bhairavgarh to Delhi was a blur of emotions for Arjun. The excitement of stepping into the bustling city was mixed with the weight of responsibility. Arjun had one goal in mind: to join the Indian Army. The city was intimidating with its towering buildings and fast-paced life, yet it felt like the perfect place to embark on the next phase of his journey. He was leaving behind the quiet lanes of Bhairavgarh, the fields where his father, Mahavir, toiled as a farmer, and the comforting routine of village life. But now, Delhi beckoned with all its challenges and opportunities.

Arjun had arranged to stay with Mahavir's distant cousin, Harvinder Rathore, who lived in Kalkaji. Harvinder, once a sprightly hockey player in his youth, had long since retired and now enjoyed a quieter life. Despite his age, Harvinder still carried himself with the same discipline he had learned on the field. He had a keen interest in fitness and had offered to help Arjun with his preparation to get into the Army. So, it was here, in this small yet peaceful corner of Delhi, that Arjun would prepare for the rigorous Army entrance exams.

The idea of joining the Army had been with Arjun for years, but he had kept it to himself, not wanting to disappoint his father, who had envisioned a different future for him. It was only when he visited Harvinder that it took shape.

One evening, while they sat on the terrace watching the sunset, Arjun found himself opening up. Harvinder asked what he planned to do after college.

Arjun hesitated, his throat tightening with the weight of unspoken words. His father's voice echoed in his mind, reminding him of the expectations. He had spent years in the shadow of those expectations, trying to convince himself that they were his own. But deep down, he knew they weren't.

Finally, the truth slipped out, unexpected but inevitable. "I want to join the Army," Arjun said, his voice barely above a whisper. As the words left his mouth, he felt a strange sense of relief mixed with an undeniable anxiety.

Harvinder was quiet for a moment as if processing what Arjun had just revealed. Then he smiled, a knowing, approving smile. "You know, Arjun," he said, his voice steady and full of warmth, "you have that same fire in you that I had when I was younger. The discipline, the drive... it's in your bones. You will make a good soldier."

Arjun's heart raced at Harvinder's words. It was as if a weight had been lifted from his chest. He had never heard anyone articulate his desire in such a way before—his quiet longing, his yearning to be a part of something bigger than himself. It was as if Harvinder had seen into his soul and recognised the hidden part of him that had always wanted more than a mundane existence.

"But I haven't told Baba," Arjun admitted, his voice catching. "He wants me to focus on studies, get a regular job, something stable."

Harvinder nodded thoughtfully, his expression softening as he considered the situation. "I understand," he said, his voice laced with empathy. "Parents want what's best for us, but sometimes, they don't see the path we're meant to walk. Sometimes, we have to follow our own path, even when it's different from what they expect of us."

Arjun looked at Harvinder, the weight of his words sinking in.

"The Army is not just a job, Arjun; it's a calling," Harvinder continued, his voice firm yet compassionate. "And if it's in your heart, you shouldn't ignore it. You'll regret it, believe me."

Those words hit Arjun deeply, like a revelation. Harvinder wasn't just offering advice—he was offering validation. For the first time, someone had recognised his inner struggle and encouraged him to follow his heart, regardless of the consequences. It was as if a door had opened, and Arjun could see, for the first time, the possibility of a future that was his to create, not dictated by anyone's expectations.

As the sunset faded into the night, Arjun sat in silence, his heart filled with a newfound resolve. He now had the courage to face his father and speak the truth, even if it meant going against the grain. He knew it wouldn't be easy, but he also knew that living a life true to himself was the only way forward. He was ready to walk his own path, no matter where it would lead.

Arjun's life in Delhi quickly settled into a routine. Enrolled at Shivaji College, his studies continued. But it was a mere backdrop to his true mission. Between attending lectures, Arjun would rush to the nearby coaching centre where he studied for the Army's entrance exam.

Harvinder, who had been a hockey player in his younger days, became an unexpected mentor in Arjun's fitness journey. Every morning, before the sun had risen, Harvinder would wake Arjun for their early morning runs.

"Wake up, Arjun! You want to join the Army, right?" Harvinder's voice would echo through the small apartment.

Arjun would groaned, pulling the blanket over his head. "Five more minutes."

"Five minutes of sleep won't get you five extra points in the exam!" Harvinder would chuckle, pulling the blanket away.

Grumbling, Arjun would get up, lace his running shoes, and follow Harvinder out into the cold morning air. The walks and runs around the Jahapanah Forest became part of their daily routine. The lush greenery, combined with the tranquillity of the early mornings, provided the perfect escape from the city's demands.

As they would jog along the winding paths, Harvinder would share stories from his past. "There was a time when I was always on the field before sunrise. I was the best striker in my college," he said, his voice tinged with nostalgia.

"Then why did you quit?" Arjun would ask, breathing heavily as he tried to keep up.

"Life has its own plans," Harvinder would shrug, never giving him the reason. "But giving up fitness is like giving up the fight. You want to outrun your friends, right?"

Arjun would wipe sweat from his forehead and nodd. "Not just my friends. I want to be the best."

Harvinder would smile. "That's the spirit. Remember, discipline today will shape your tomorrow."

Arjun would laugh. "One day, when I wear the uniform, I'll make you run with me!"

"I'll be proud to," Harvinder would grin. "But for now, run faster!"

Arjun pushed himself harder, every day, his determination growing with every step. The road ahead was long, but with Harvinder's guidance, he knew he was on the right path.

On the days when Harvinder wasn't able to join him, Arjun would continue the runs alone. The 'forest', with its ancient trees and quiet ambience, became his sanctuary. The physical exertion and the mental focus he developed during these runs helped him maintain a balance in his preparation. The early mornings were his time to clear his mind, while the rest of the day was dedicated to his studies.

Arjun always knew that the journey to joining the Indian Army would demand every ounce of his determination. The path was clear but challenging—first, a written exam, and then the formidable Service Selection Board (SSB) interview. Both phases tested not only one's knowledge and skills but also the grit and passion required to serve the nation.

The written exam was rigorous. Arjun immersed himself in preparation, pouring over current affairs, solving intricate math problems, and expanding his vocabulary. His evenings were consumed by coaching classes, and his nights were spent reviewing notes. Balancing his college work and Army preparation demanded discipline, but Arjun thrived on the challenge.

Yet, it was the SSB interview that loomed largest in his mind. He had heard countless stories about the punishing physical tasks, psychological evaluations, and leadership tests designed to push candidates to their limits. Arjun envisioned himself not just excelling but embodying the qualities of courage and resilience that the Army sought.

As he stayed up late once again, revising for the hundredth time, Arjun felt a quiet determination. This was not just an exam—it was the gateway to a lifelong dream.

And amidst all this, there were phone calls between him and his parents. They used to ask about college, and he would assure them that all was fine despite the weight of the pressure he was under.

Harvinder always egged him on, urging him to tell his father the truth, but Arjun couldn't bring himself to do it. There was something inside him that held him back, a feeling he couldn't quite name. Perhaps it was his desire to shield his father from any worry or disappointment.

Then, one afternoon, just a week before the exam, something happened that made Arjun open up to his father. It was a typical college day. Arjun had just finished a lecture and was walking across campus when he overheard a hushed conversation near the student bulletin board. A group of students stood in a circle, their expressions sombre. "Did you hear? Prerna... Prerna from the literature department... she took her life yesterday."

Arjun froze, the words hitting him like a punch to the gut. Prerna? She was always so bright, so full of potential. The shock was overwhelming, but what struck him more was the whisper that followed.

"She was being forced into marriage," one student murmured. "She didn't want it. She wanted to study, to make something of herself. But her parents... they had already arranged her marriage. They said it was time."

The realisation hit Arjun hard. He had always known that the pressures of family expectations could be suffocating for some, but hearing Prerna's story—her dreams cut short, her voice silenced by a decision that wasn't hers—shook him deeply. It made him reflect on his own situation, where he had been holding back his dreams to shield his father from disappointment.

Arjun felt a surge of emotion. He couldn't keep pretending that he was okay with the path he was on if it wasn't truly his. He couldn't let fear or expectations dictate his future, just as Prerna couldn't. He had to take control of his life, just as she had wished she could do before it was too late.

He left the campus that day in a daze, his thoughts a whirlwind of emotions. For the first time in months, the pressure of keeping his Army dream a secret seemed unbearable. He needed to be honest with his father, to share his true calling, not just for himself but for the memory of Prerna, whose dreams had been stolen from her.

By the time he got home, his heart was set. He couldn't keep pretending anymore. Without hesitation, he dialled his father's number. As the phone at the other end rang thoughts raced through his mind. What if his father didn't understand? What if he was disappointed? He was nervous, but he knew he could no longer ignore the truth.

"Baba," Arjun's voice wavered when his father picked up. "I... I need to talk to you...kuch batana hai."

His father's voice was warm, but there was a softness in it that Arjun hadn't expected. "Haan beta, bilkul. Kya baat hai?"[11]

Arjun struggled to find the words. He wanted to say it all at once, but it felt impossible. His throat tightened as he hesitated, the weight of his secret pressing down on him.

"Baba, yeh... yeh college ke baare mein hai. Main... main soch raha hoon... aur mujhe ab nahi lagta ki main sahi raste par hoon."[12]

His father's voice was gentle, yet there was an insistence in it. "Kya matlab, Arjun? Tum hamesha apne padhayi mein achha karte ho. Tum mein kitni kshamata hai. Kya pareshani ho gayi hai?"[13]

Arjun exhaled shakily, feeling the lump in his throat. "Baba, yeh padhayi ke baare mein nahi hai... yeh uske baad ke baare mein hai. Main... main Army ke liye tayari kar raha hoon. Exam ki. Aur mujhe lagta hai... mujhe lagta hai ki wahi mera asli raasta hai. Yeh college nahi. Main yeh dikhawa aur zyada nahi kar sakta."[14]

There was a long pause on the other end of the line. Arjun could almost hear the thoughts swirling in his father's mind. Was he disappointed? Was he angry?

Then, in a quiet but firm voice, his father spoke. "Arjun, main jaanta hoon ki tum hamesha alag the. Jab se tum chhote the, tum mein ek junoon tha, ek iraada tha. Main hamesha use dekh raha tha, chahe tumne khud kabhi usse mehsoos nahi kiya. Lekin..."[15] His father sighed softly and continued. "Yeh mere liye asaan nahi hai. Mere liye kuch alag plans the. Main chahta tha ki tum ek surakshit raasta apnaao. Par main tumhe kuch banne ke liye majboor nahi kar sakta jo tum nahi ho."[16]

Arjun's heart pounded, the words he had feared hearing hanging in the air. He braced himself, expecting the worst. But then his father continued, his voice filled with pride.

"Arjun, main tumpar garv karta hoon. Tumne mere saath imandari se baat ki, aur apna raasta chuna. Main chahta tha ki tum hamesha apne dil ki suno. Agar Army wahi jagah hai jahan tumhe hona chahiye, toh jao. Main tumhara saath dunga. Yeh woh zindagi nahi thi jo maine tumhare liye sochi thi, par yeh tumhari zindagi hai. Aur yeh mere liye sab kuch hai."[17]

Tears welled up in Arjun's eyes, a mix of relief and gratitude flooding through him. "Baba... shukriya. Mujhe itna dar lag raha tha aapse yeh kehne ka. Mujhe nahi pata tha aap kaise react karoge."[18]

His father chuckled softly, the sound full of warmth. "Maine tumhe badhte hue dekha hai, Arjun. Tum mein wahi junoon hai jo kabhi mujhme tha. Tum hamesha jaante the ki tumhe kya chahiye, chahe main samajh na paaya hoon. Ab waqt hai apne sapne ka peecha karne ka. Kuch bhi tumhe rokne mat dena."[19]

Arjun's chest tightened with emotion. For the first time in years, he felt truly understood. His father wasn't just accepting his decision; he was proud of him for making it.

"Main tumhe garv mehsoos karvaunga, Baba,"[20] Arjun whispered, feeling a sense of purpose settle over him.

"Main jaanta hoon beta. Main jaanta hoon,"[21] his father replied.

As Arjun ended the call, he finally felt a weight lift off his shoulders. He was no longer afraid to follow his calling. He was ready to step forward, knowing his father's support would always be with him.

As the exam date drew closer, Arjun's nerves grew. But he reminded himself that this was the culmination of everything he had worked for. His time in Delhi had been a whirlwind of classes, coaching, and fitness training, but it had also been filled with moments of self-discovery. He wasn't just preparing for an exam; he was preparing to become the man he had always wanted to be—the man who could serve his country with honour and pride.

On the morning of the written exam, Arjun felt the familiar knot of anxiety in his stomach. But he pushed it aside, just as Harvinder had taught him to push through the fatigue during their runs. The exam hall was packed, and the tension in the air was palpable. When the papers were handed out, Arjun took a deep breath and focused, reading each question carefully. By the end of the exam, Arjun was exhausted but relieved. He had done his best. He received the results after some weeks. He had cleared the written exam with a good score. The real challenge awaited him though—the SSB interview. The selection process was known for its intensity, and he was mentally prepared for it. The first part of the SSB was the group discussion. Arjun had practised with Harvinder and his friends, discussing everything from national issues to global conflicts. During the group discussion, Arjun took a backseat initially, letting others express their opinions, but when the moment came, he spoke confidently, making sure his ideas were heard. Next came the psychological tests, which were designed to assess a candidate's mental strength. These tests included word association and story writing, where Arjun had to think quickly and respond without hesitation. The resilience he had built since his childhood helped him face the challenge with unwavering determination. The physical fitness test was another arduous part of the SSB. Arjun had prepared for this through months of training, and he was in peak physical condition. The pull-ups, push-ups, and running tests felt like second nature to him. His body had become a reflection of the discipline he had followed in the months leading up to the exam.

On the final day, Arjun faced the personal interview. The officers asked him about his family, his aspirations, and why he wanted to join the Army. Arjun answered honestly, speaking about the values of discipline and service that had been instilled in him by his father, Mahavir. He told them about his upbringing as a farmer's son, his love for his country, and his desire to serve in the Army. And, of course, he did not forget to mention the strength of his mother. She was not just a homemaker or a housewife; she was the foundation of his resilience. Often, we focus so much on the father's role that the mother's sacrifices remain unnoticed, but Arjun saw things differently. He had watched his mother fight silent battles, endure hardships, and still offer warmth and wisdom with a steady heart. She was his first teacher, his quiet protector, and the reason he learned to stand tall even in the face of storms. For Arjun, his mother was not just a presence in the background—she was the force that shaped his very being.

When the final results were announced, he was ecstatic. He had cleared the SSB and had been selected to join the National Defence Academy (NDA) for training. It was the moment he had worked so hard for, and though the journey had been long and filled with obstacles, he had made it.

When the acceptance letter finally arrived, Arjun called home, his voice trembling with emotion. He said. "Baba, I'm going to be a soldier."

Mahavir's silence on the other end spoke volumes.

When he finally spoke, his voice was thick with pride. "Mujhe hamesha pata tha, Arjun."[22]

He could hear his mother in the background, echoing the same words. Arjun shut his eyes and imagined the scene—his mother clutching the pallu of her sari, fighting back tears of joy, while his father let his own fall freely. Without a doubt, the diya would be lit under the tulsi plant as soon as he hung up. He missed home. But his journey to protect a greater home—his nation—had begun.

A few days later, as he stood on the platform, ready to board the train to Pune, Arjun felt a deep sense of pride. Delhi had been the starting point, but the true test was ahead of him. The NDA was where his transformation would take place. Arjun knew that this was just the beginning of his journey toward becoming the man he had always dreamed of being—a soldier in the Indian Army.

***

[1]"Who was that man?"

[2]"A protector of our nation."

[3]"You're always helping others,"

[4]"It's a rare quality, Arjun. Hold onto it."

[5]"Son, you saved us today."

[6]"This is your chance, beta,"

[7]"Make us proud."

[8]"You will do well, Arjun,"

[9]"But remember, strength comes from within. The world will test you, but never forget who you are."

[10]"Take care of yourself, Arjun. And remember, no matter where you go, we are always with you."

[11]"Yes, sure. What is the matter?"

[12]"Baba, this... this is about college. I... I've been thinking... and now I don't feel like I'm on the right path."

[13]"What do you mean, Arjun? You always do well in your studies. You have so much potential. What's wrong?"

[14]"Baba, this isn't about studies... it's about what comes after. I... I'm preparing for the Army. For the exam. And I think... I think that's my true path. Not this college. I can't keep up this pretense any longer."

[15]"Arjun, I know that you have always been different. Ever since you were a child, there was a passion in you, a determination. I have always seen it, even if you never felt it yourself. But..."

[16]"This is not easy for me. I had different plans. I wanted you to take a safe path. But I cannot force you to become something you are not."

[17]"Arjun, I am proud of you. You spoke to me honestly and chose your own path. I always wanted you to follow your heart. If the Army is where you truly belong, then go. I will stand by you. This is not the life I had envisioned for you, but it is your life. And that means everything to me."

[18]"Baba... thank you. I was so scared to say this to you. I didn't know how you would react."

[19]"I have seen you grow, Arjun. You have the same passion that I once had. You always knew what you wanted, even if I couldn't understand it. Now is the time to chase your dream. Don't let anything stop you."

[20]"I will make you feel proud, Baba."

[21]"I know, my child. I know."

[22]"I always knew, Arjun."

CHAPTER TWO

LIFE AT IMA

Arjun's journey through the NDA was transformative. The rigorous training, intense physical challenges, and demanding academics shaped him into a disciplined and resilient individual. However, it was through these challenges that he learned the true meaning of dedication, leadership, and resilience. The hardships were not just physical; they shaped his character, teaching him to handle pressure and adversity with grace. Over time, Arjun transformed from a hopeful cadet into a disciplined individual, ready to face the responsibilities of an officer in the Indian Army.

The passing out parade marked the culmination of all his hard work. It was an emotional moment for Arjun, his family, and his friends. It symbolised the end of one chapter and the beginning of another. As he marched with his fellow cadets, his heart swelled with pride, knowing that the training, discipline, and values he had gained at NDA had prepared him for the next stage of his journey. Arjun's thoughts turned to his family—his parents, who had supported him every step of the way, and Harvinder uncle, who had been a mentor and guiding force.

His father looked on with pride, understanding the significance of the moment more than anyone. His mother watched her son with tears in her eyes, knowing that this was only the beginning of his journey as an officer. Harvinder Uncle, standing beside them, was a reminder of the importance of family and mentorship in shaping Arjun's path. It was because of him that Arjun's parents had stepped out of Bhairavgarh for the first time, their first journey on a train marked by awe, nervousness, and an unspoken determination to see their son march into his future.

Arjun knew he could never truly repay his uncle for what he had done—guiding him, supporting him, and now making sure his parents could witness this defining moment. As for his parents, they had left behind the familiar comfort of their small village, stepping into an unfamiliar world for him. And in their eyes, he saw not just pride, but the quiet acceptance that their son's destiny now lay beyond the home they had built for him. With the parade behind him, Arjun was ready for the next chapter—the Indian Military Academy (IMA).

It was the summer of 1994 when Arjun first set foot at the IMA, the hallowed grounds where countless young men were moulded into leaders of the Indian Army. As he stepped through the iconic Chetwode Hall gates, a sense of history and purpose swept over him. This was the place where Field Marshal Sam Manekshaw had once walked, honing the leadership skills that would guide India to victory in the 1971 war. Arjun couldn't help but feel a surge of pride as he imagined himself contributing to the legacy of men like General K. M. Cariappa, who had laid the foundation of the modern Indian Army as its first Commander-in-Chief. The sprawling campus seemed alive with stories of courage. Every corridor, every parade ground echoed with tales of bravery, like those of Major Somnath Sharma, the first recipient of the Param Vir Chakra, who had defended Kashmir in 1947 with unparalleled grit. Arjun would often find himself drawn to the photographs of these heroes in the mess hall

The IMA, with its sprawling grounds and imposing buildings, seemed like a world of its own, standing as a testament to the legacy of the Indian Army. The lush, green fields stretched endlessly, surrounded by towering trees that whispered stories of the cadets who had trained there before. The architecture was grand and regal, with colonial-era structures and modern facilities coexisting in harmony, each corner echoing the footsteps of those who had walked this path of discipline and honour. The atmosphere was charged with an energy that could only come from an institution dedicated to shaping the future leaders of the nation. The academy, nestled in the scenic hills of Dehradun, felt like a sanctuary of strength and purpose, where every inch of land was imbued with the spirit of service and sacrifice. It was a world Arjun had dreamed of entering for years.

Arjun was taller than most of the cadets, with broad shoulders that hinted at the strength he had built over years of hard work on his father's farm. His skin, sun-kissed, glistened in the morning sun as he stood among other young men, all eager to prove their worth. His dark, intense eyes reflected the fire within him, a fire that would carry him through the trials that lay ahead.

But despite his physical strength, Arjun knew the path would not be easy. IMA wasn't just about physical training; it was about moulding a cadet into an officer who could lead men into battle, make life-and-death decisions, and uphold the dignity of the Indian Army. The training was backbreaking, and Arjun quickly learned that nothing came easy here.

The mornings began before the first light of dawn. The sound of the bugle would cut through the stillness, urging the cadets to rise from their beds and begin their day. Arjun had always woken up early, but the cold Dehradun mornings were different—there was no time for hesitation. His body, still not used to the relentless pace of academy life, would ache from the previous day's training. But there was no room for weakness. He had come here for one reason: to serve his country, and to do that, he needed to push past the pain.

The physical drills were brutal. Running up hills, crawling under barbed wire, scaling walls—these were the tasks that faced them every morning. Arjun's legs would burn as he sprinted up the slopes, the wind biting at his face. His chest would tighten with the effort, but he would push through, his breath ragged, his focus unwavering. The trainers, with their harsh voices and unforgiving manner, seemed to take a special interest in him. "Faster, Arjun! Don't you dare stop now!" they would shout as if the very essence of his being depended on that last push. And Arjun did push.

One morning, during the infamous 'obstacle course', Arjun found himself struggling with a particularly difficult task—a massive wall that stood imposingly in front of him. He had done it before, but today, his body felt heavier, his muscles sore from the previous day's demanding drills. As he approached the wall, he glanced sideways to see Raghav, one who went on to become one of his closest friends, already preparing to scale it. He knew Raghav was a natural athlete, but Arjun had always prided himself on pushing past his limits, even when it seemed impossible.

With a deep breath, Arjun took a running start, launching himself toward the wall. His fingers barely caught the edge, but it was enough. For a moment, he hung there, his legs dangling, his heart pounding.

"Come on, Arjun!" Raghav shouted from below, urging him on.

Arjun gritted his teeth, pulling himself upward with every ounce of strength he had left. His arms burned, his fingers ached, but his resolve never wavered. He reached the top, pulled himself over, and slid down the other side, landing with a triumphant smile. The trainers, though stern, couldn't hide a small glimmer of approval in their eyes.

But, of course, no story of Arjun at IMA would be complete without a bit of humour. During one particularly intense morning session, the cadets were tasked with completing a five-kilometre run in under 30 minutes. Arjun, ever the competitor, pushed himself to the limit. He was a few meters from the finish line when he spotted Sameer, a cadet known for his less-than-stellar running skills, struggling behind. Sameer had always been more of a thinker than an athlete, and on this morning, he was gasping for air, his face beet-red.

Without a second thought, Arjun slowed down just enough to make sure Sameer caught up to him.

"Come on, Sameer! You've got this!" Arjun yelled over his shoulder, encouraging his friend.

Sameer, though barely able to breathe, managed to pick up the pace. But just as he was about to pass Arjun, he tripped over a stone, tumbling in a spectacular fashion right into a muddy puddle. Mud splattered everywhere—on Sameer, on Arjun, and even on the trainers who were watching from the side-lines.

The trainers couldn't help but burst into laughter, and Sameer, face flushed with embarrassment, scrambled to his feet. "I swear, Arjun, you jinxed me!" he groaned.

Arjun, laughing, reached out a hand to help him up. "Hey, you ran your best time yet!"

Arjun's teasing earned a playful shove from Sameer. The trainers, still chuckling, gave them both a few words of encouragement, reminding them that at IMA, it wasn't just about the physical strength but the ability to endure and support each other through the toughest moments.

This was the essence of IMA—where the boundaries of physical endurance were tested, but companionship and humour helped the cadets keep going. Even in the most challenging moments, Arjun learned that strength wasn't just about pushing yourself to the limit; it was about lifting each other up, even when you were covered in mud or struggling to catch your breath.

But it wasn't just physical endurance that mattered here—it was mental toughness. For every drop of sweat that fell from his brow, there was a voice in his head telling him to stop, to rest, to take a breather. But Arjun had learned early on that there was no room for weakness in the academy. His resolve was tested with every drill, every exercise, every moment of exhaustion. He would dig deep, drawing from his inner strength, and push himself further.

The intensity of the training was matched only by the emotional toll it took on him. Arjun missed home more than he had anticipated. It seemed like a lifetime away. He missed the smell of the earth after a fresh rainfall, the sound of his father's voice as they worked the fields together, and the quiet companionship he shared with his mother.

Through the toiling days at IMA, Arjun found solace in the friendships he formed. He bonded with Raghav. Raghav was the kind of person who wore his heart on his sleeve, and Arjun admired him for it. They would often train together, pushing each other to run faster, climb higher, and endure more. There was a kinship between them that made the pain more bearable. Then there was Sameer, who had a sharp wit and a sense of humour that helped lighten the mood after the most tiring exercises. Sameer had an infectious laugh, and his ability to make light of even the toughest situations made him a favourite among the cadets. Together, the trio became inseparable, and their bond was solidified during their time at IMA.

The trio quickly earned a reputation at the mess. They were known for their constant chatter, their shared jokes, and their loud laughter that echoed across the dining hall. In a place where discipline and structure were paramount, the mess became their sanctuary—a place where they could unwind, joke around, and forget about the endless drills for a while. Arjun, Raghav, and Sameer became the heart of the mess, with their antics providing a much-needed break for the other cadets.

There was one night when the three of them decided to stay up well past the allotted lights-out time. The moonlight filtered through the windows of their barracks, casting long shadows on the walls. As the others fell asleep, Arjun, Raghav, and Sameer lay awake in their beds, whispering and laughing quietly. They spoke about everything—life before IMA, their dreams for the future, and sometimes, just the absurdities of the world they had been thrown into.

Sameer, with his knack for humour, kept the conversation going. "You know, guys, I was thinking the other day..." he began, his voice a conspiratorial whisper, "If we could survive all these drills, we could probably handle anything. I mean, the next time someone tries to rob a bank, we'll just show up and make them run five kilometres. That'll teach them a lesson!"

Raghav chuckled softly, but Arjun, always the more serious one, shook his head. "You're crazy, Sameer. But it's true. This place... it changes us. You come out of this place stronger, not just physically, but mentally too."

Sameer, ever the optimist, added, "Well, I don't know about mentally strong, but I'm definitely getting stronger in dodging mud puddles and scaling walls. And with the way you two run, maybe we can win a relay race at the Olympics!"

The three burst into laughter, the sound ringing out in the quiet barracks, the kind of laughter only friends who had been through hardship together could share. They spent hours that night talking, plotting their future lives as officers, and making jokes about the ridiculous things they had to endure at IMA.

One day, during a particularly tiring exercise, they found themselves at the end of a long training session, exhausted and covered in sweat. That's when Raghav had an idea—a mischievous idea, as usual. "I bet you guys I can get out of doing today's punishment," he said with a grin, his eyes gleaming. "All I need is a little bit of charm, and those trainers won't even know what hit them."

Arjun and Sameer exchanged sceptical glances, but Sameer was confident. He strutted up to the training officer, who had just announced the punishment drill for the day. With a grin that could melt ice, Raghav began his act, pretending to be in a state of complete exhaustion.

"Sir, I am absolutely spent, I don't think I can give my 100 per cent today," he said, putting on his best 'sick cadet' voice. "I think I'm coming down with something. Maybe I should rest, Sir."

The officer, who had seen it all before, raised an eyebrow. "Rest? You want to rest after every drill, Raghav?" the officer barked.

But he didn't back down. He continued to plead, his performance almost convincing enough to make even Arjun feel sorry for him.

Finally, the officer sighed and said, "Fine. You can rest for today—but only because I don't want to deal with your theatrics."

As soon as Raghav returned to the group, Sameer and Arjun burst into laughter. "You really pulled that off?" Arjun asked, shaking his head in disbelief.

Raghav grinned widely. "Never underestimate the power of a good performance, my friends," he said, as if he had just won a great battle.

From that day on, the trio was known as the 'Tri-Veer' of IMA, but they never let their mischief get in the way of their training. In the midst of the hardships and discipline of Army life, it was these moments—these bonds—that made their journey memorable. They learned that strength wasn't just about physical endurance; it was about finding joy in the little things, about lifting each other up during the hardest days, and about never losing sight of the humour that helped them get through it all.

Arjun found comfort in their friendship, in the way they supported each other through the long days and nights. Their bond was unbreakable, a brotherhood forged in the fires of training.

One evening, after a particularly exhausting day, the three of them sat together on the edge of the barracks, looking out at the distant hills. The air was thick with the scent of pine, and the sky above them was painted in shades of orange and pink as the sun began to set.

"Arjun, you're going to be a great officer," Sameer said, his voice full of genuine admiration. "I can see it in the way you lead us, even when things get tough."

Arjun smiled but didn't respond immediately. Sameer's words felt like a heavy weight on his chest. He wasn't sure if he was ready for what lay ahead, but he knew he couldn't back down now. He had come too far.

Raghav chuckled softly. "You're both talking like we've already graduated. Let's get through tomorrow's drill first, eh?"

The joke lightened the mood, but Arjun couldn't shake the weight of the responsibility that loomed over him. Each day at IMA felt like a test, each drill a new challenge, and with every passing day, Arjun felt himself growing stronger, not just physically but mentally as well.

His leadership skills began to take shape, tested in the most extreme of circumstances. During one particularly harrowing exercise in the field, Arjun had to lead his team through a simulated combat situation. The terrain was difficult, and the weather had turned cold and wet. The team was exhausted, and morale was low. Arjun could see it in the eyes of his men—the weariness, the doubt. Yet, he knew that as their leader, it was his job to lift them up, to remind them of why they were here.

"Listen up, everyone!" Arjun shouted over the howling wind. "We've trained for this. We don't quit. Not here, not now. We push through together, or we don't push through at all."

His words rang out with a confidence that surprised even him. There was something about leading others that ignited a fire in him, a fire that had always been there but had never been tested this fiercely. The team rallied behind him, their spirits lifted by his resolve. They finished the exercise as a unit, their tired bodies moving with renewed purpose.

As the weeks passed, Arjun's transformation was evident. His physical strength, once a result of hard labour, was now honed by disciplined training. His leadership, forged in the heat of intense drills, was becoming more natural, more assured. His peers respected him, and his instructors began to take notice of his unwavering determination and his ability to lead under pressure.

But the emotional toll of IMA was not easily forgotten. There were nights when Arjun lay awake in his barracks, staring up at the ceiling, thinking about his father, wondering if he would ever live up to the man's expectations. He knew his father would be proud, but Arjun also knew the weight of the responsibility he carried. He wasn't just representing himself; he was representing his family, his village, and the values that had been instilled in him since childhood.

When Arjun would approach his final month at IMA, he would begin to reflect on the person he had become. The cadet who had arrived at the academy full of uncertainty and doubt was now a confident, determined young man ready to take on the world. He had forged lifelong friendships, learned to lead with compassion and strength, and, most importantly, had learned to trust in himself.

The day of his graduation, the passing-out parade, would be a day of both celebration and reflection. Arjun would stand tall with his fellow cadets, his chest swelling with pride as he looked out over the parade ground. The academy would have shaped him and tested him in ways he would have never imagined, but would emerge stronger, more resilient, and more determined than ever.

As the Commandant of the academy would address the cadets, Arjun's thoughts would drift back to his father's words: *"Humein garv mehsoos karwao, Arjun."*[1] He would know he had done just that. The journey ahead would be challenging, but he would be ready. The man who had arrived at IMA as a boy would have become an officer—a leader—and nothing would be able to stand in his way.

***

[1] "Make us proud, Arjun."

CHAPTER THREE

MEERA'S 'MOHAN'

Arjun's leave was a rare luxury, one that he had been eagerly anticipating. After months of rigorous training and discipline at the IMA, he finally had time to unwind. The countryside of Bhairavgarh had offered him peace, but it was the vibrant chaos of Jaipur that had been calling to him. He had planned a holiday with Sameer, hoping to recharge before returning to the academy, but little did he know that Jaipur would hold something more than just a break from his routine.

They were walking through a mall, a far cry from the usual military barracks, with Sameer happily distracted by the latest gadgets and Arjun, almost reluctantly, following along. His mind kept wandering back to the early morning drills and the constant demand for perfection, but the noise of the mall was a welcome distraction. Arjun appreciated the moments of calmness—moments that felt distant from the harsh, demanding life he led at IMA.

As they passed a bookstore, his eyes caught sight of her. Meera (as he would know later). She was standing near the entrance, surrounded by a group of friends, but it was her laughter that pulled him in. Her laughter wasn't just a sound, it was an energy that filled the space, light and unrestrained, making the world around her seem just a little brighter. The way she tilted her head back, her eyes closing briefly as she laughed, was something Arjun couldn't ignore.

He tried to look away, but there was something magnetic about her presence. It wasn't just her smile or the way her dark curls framed her face, but the aura of warmth and confidence she carried. Arjun found himself unintentionally pausing. His heart rate picked up, and for a moment, he could have sworn the world around him slowed. Sameer, noticing Arjun's sudden pause, nudged him with an amused smirk.

Arjun snapped out of his daze, trying to hide his discomfort. "It's nothing. Just... just looking around," he muttered, trying to sound casual, though his voice betrayed him. Sameer followed his view and immediately understood.

"Ohhh, I see," Sameer said, his eyes widening comically. "Aha! She's the one, huh?"

Arjun rolled his eyes, shifting his feet uncomfortably. "What do you mean, 'the one'? She's just a woman in a bookstore."

Sameer grinned mischievously. "Just a woman, huh? She's just standing there, minding her own business, and you're practically melting. Arjun, my friend, I think we have a classic case of love at first sight!"

Arjun shot him a glare. "Don't be ridiculous. I'm not... I'm not melting."

"Sure you're not," Sameer said, winking. He crossed his arms and leaned against the nearby pillar, adopting a dramatic stance. "Listen, if you want to talk to her, you have to make a move, man."

Arjun's heart skipped a beat, and he instinctively rubbed the back of his neck. He had never been good at talking to women—especially not in such a spontaneous, unexpected setting. His life, up until now, had been consumed by discipline, drills, and rigorous training. The most significant interaction he had with women was usually reserved for his family or a few occasional conversations with classmates. And even those, he never quite knew how to navigate.

"Make a move?" Arjun repeated, his voice dripping with scepticism. "What am I supposed to do, walk up and say, 'Hey, I'm Arjun. You're the most beautiful woman I've ever seen in a bookstore'?"

Sameer laughed loudly. "Nah, man! Bollywood style. You have to be smooth. Tell her, 'Aapke chehre par ek raaz hai.'[1] Something mysterious. It's all about the charm, bro."

Arjun stared at Sameer, baffled. "What?"

Sameer grinned wider, clearly enjoying himself. "Trust me, dude. It works in the movies."

Arjun raised an eyebrow. "Sameer, you think I'm going to walk up to a woman and recite such cheesy lines?"

Sameer leaned closer, lowering his voice dramatically. "Of course, Arjun. Women love that stuff. You just have to say it with confidence, like you know what you're doing."

Arjun groaned, running a hand through his hair. "I don't know... this feels different. This isn't some movie where I just walk up, say some nonsense, and the girl falls for me."

Sameer's eyes twinkled with mischief. "Well, how else do you think it happens? You have to put yourself out there, man! You're going to become a Lieutenant, for God's sake. Women love a man in uniform. All you have to do is be bold. You've faced worse situations, right? A little conversation won't kill you."

Arjun looked at Sameer in disbelief. "You think that's all it takes? A few cheesy lines and a uniform? And, anyway we are not in our uniforms. How would she even know?"

Before Sameer could answer, Arjun looked back at the bookstore, and that's when he saw her look up from the book she had been reading. Their eyes met, and for a brief moment, the world around them seemed to shrink. Time seemed to stretch out. His heart skipped, and he felt a rush of warmth spread through him.

Meera's glance lingered on him for a fraction of a second longer than necessary, and then, as if on cue, she tucked a stray lock of hair behind her ear. Arjun's breath caught in his throat. It was such an effortless, natural gesture—simple, but it made his heart race even more. In that instant, he knew it wasn't just the books or the uniform that had made him stop—it was her.

"Arjun!" Sameer's voice broke through his thoughts. "She's looking right at you, man! This is your chance!"

Arjun turned to face his friend, his mind a blur of thoughts. He could feel the pulse of adrenaline in his veins. His hands felt clammy. This wasn't a military operation. This wasn't something he could train for. It was just him, standing in front of a woman who had caught his attention in a way that felt entirely unfamiliar.

"Go on, man. Don't let the moment slip away," Sameer urged.

Arjun swallowed hard. He knew he couldn't stand here forever. If he didn't make a move now, he would regret it. Taking a deep breath, he straightened his posture, adjusting his uniform. He looked one last time at Meera, who was still looking at him, her expression a mixture of curiosity and amusement.

"Alright," Arjun muttered, more to himself than Sameer. "Here goes nothing."

Sameer slapped him on the back with a chuckle. "Good luck, Lieutenant!"

Arjun nodded, giving his friend a half-smile before turning toward the bookstore. His palms were sweaty, his heart thudding in his chest, but there was a strange sense of resolve that pushed him forward. It wasn't about Bollywood lines or trying to impress her. It was about being genuine.

As he walked closer, he could feel the nerves bubbling in his stomach. He had no idea what to say, but he was going to try. He wasn't the type to approach strangers, especially someone like her. His life had always been about discipline, goals, and strict routines. He wasn't used to spontaneous moments like this. But there was something about her that made him forget his usual reserve. He could not just let this pass by.

As he moved closer, his mind started to race. He hadn't spoken to many women outside his family and a few friends, and in the controlled environment of IMA, those encounters were few and far between. He had always considered himself a man of focus, someone who didn't waste time on distractions. But now, standing at the edge of the bookstore, staring at Meera, as he would find out later, he began to question himself. Should he even approach her? He had read about how soldiers, especially officers, were admired for their discipline and stoicism. But it was different in reality. He had no idea how to even begin a conversation.

"Arjun, you've got this," he muttered under his breath, feeling the weight of his uniform, the very uniform that had instilled confidence in him for so long. He could face any challenge the army threw at him, so why should talking to a woman be any different?

Just then, Sameer's voice interrupted his thoughts. He had followed Arjun and now stood beside him, watching Meera from a distance. "Dude, you're overthinking this," Sameer said, nudging him lightly. "Just go up to her. What's the worst that can happen?"

Arjun looked at Sameer, still unsure. "I don't know, Sameer. What if I mess up? What if I say something stupid?"

"Relax," Sameer said with a grin. "You've got that uniform on, right? Just throw in a few Bollywood movie lines. You know, the typical stuff—'Are you a magician? Because every time I look at you, everyone else disappears.'"

Arjun turned to him, his face blank. "What?" he asked incredulously.

"Trust me, bro," Sameer said, shrugging and grinning. "Such lines work magic. You'll have her eating out of your hand."

Arjun stared at him, his mind racing. Bollywood? He had only watched a handful of movies, and they had taught him nothing about real-life interaction. "Sameer, you do realise that's the worst advice I've ever heard, right?"

Sameer laughed, slapping Arjun on the back. "You're overthinking, man. Just go for it."

Arjun stood; immobile. Still unsure. Was he really going to use a cheesy Bollywood line on a woman like her? She seemed so... sophisticated. He wasn't sure if the 'magician' line would work on someone like her.

But as if fate had decided for him, Meera turned slightly, catching his look. For a split second, their eyes locked—her curious, warm eyes meeting his, and in that instant, his heart skipped a beat. She smiled faintly, and then, with a graceful movement, she tucked a stray lock of hair behind her ear. It was such a simple gesture, but it sent a jolt through him, and suddenly, everything felt clear.

She had noticed him.

Arjun's breath caught in his throat. His instincts took over. He could either stand there, paralysed by uncertainty, or he could seize the moment. His chest tightened, and with a deep breath, he stepped forward, closing the space between them. Sameer gave him a quick thumbs-up, but Arjun barely registered it.

As he reached her, his voice came out a little more nervous than he intended, but he pushed through. "Ma'am... Excuse me," he began, his hands slightly trembling. "Are you always this happy, or is it the books that bring out your smile?"

Meera turned to him, a playful glint in her eyes. She raised an eyebrow, as if she had been expecting this moment.

"That depends," she said, her voice laced with amusement. "Are you always this forward, or is it the uniform that gives you courage?"

Arjun blinked in surprise. "Uniform? What uniform?"

He wasn't wearing one. How did she know?

Meera smirked. "Why? Aren't you a soldier?"

He stared at her, stunned. "How did you know?"

She simply pointed to his crew-cut hair. "This. And the way you addressed me as 'Ma'am'. It gave you away."

A slow smile spread across Arjun's face. "You're very observant, Ma'am," he said, emphasising the last word deliberately. His confidence was returning, bit by bit. "I don't usually approach strangers, but you seemed... interesting."

Meera's eyes sparkled as she tilted her head. "Well," she said with a smirk, "I wasn't expecting to be approached by someone in uniform at a bookstore."

Arjun chuckled. "I wasn't expecting to find someone as radiant as you either." He paused, feeling the 'cringy' words come before he could stop them. "I mean, your smile caught my attention. It's hard to ignore someone who lights up a place just by being here."

Meera raised an eyebrow, clearly amused. "Flattery works, I see. But I've heard that line before."

"Well, maybe it's true," Arjun replied. "But I'll be honest, I don't usually go around handing out compliments."

"Then I must be special," Meera teased, her smile widening.

"Well, I wouldn't say that..." Arjun started, but before he could continue, Meera's group of friends called out to her.

Meera glanced back at her friends, then returned her view to Arjun. "I should probably get back to my friends," she said, "But it was nice to meet you...Lieutenant?"

Arjun replied, "To be..." They were both silent for a few seconds before he added, "I wouldn't want to keep you from your friends. But..." He hesitated for a moment, then continued, "Maybe we could continue this conversation sometime?"

Meera's smile softened, her eyes thoughtful. "I'd like that," she said, her voice genuine. "I'll be around. Maybe we'll bump into each other again."

Sameer, who had been watching from a distance, joined him with a raised eyebrow. "Well, well, looks like someone got the courage to talk to a beautiful woman. What did I miss?"

Arjun barely heard Sameer's teasing as her parting words replayed in his mind. "Maybe we'll bump into each other again." The way she said it, soft and sincere, had struck a chord. She didn't offer a number, a way to contact her, nothing—just a warm smile and a glimmer of hope.

Sameer said, waving a hand in front of his friend's face, "You look like someone who just won the lottery but misplaced the ticket. What's the plan? Or are you planning to just stand here until she materialises again?"

Arjun blinked, finally registering Sameer's words. "What? No. I mean, I don't know. We just... talked. She said we might bump into each other again."

"That's it?" Sameer's eyebrows shot up. "No number? No carrier pigeon address?"

"No," Arjun admitted, his grin faltering. "But it felt... natural. Like it wasn't the end of something but the start of..."

Sameer cut him off with a mock gasp. "Oh no. He's gone full poet. Quick, someone call the emergency services. My friend has been struck by the lightning of loooove."

Arjun shoved him lightly, a sheepish smile on his face. "Shut up, man. You weren't there. There was a... connection."

"Ah, yes. The mystical connection. Did the universe align? Did birds sing? Did violins play softly in the background?"

"Forget it," Arjun muttered, walking ahead. Sameer followed, still grinning.

They reached the café where they had planned to grab a coffee. Arjun, still distracted, ordered without thinking and sat by the window, his stare drifting to the street outside.

Sameer, never one to let a moment of teasing go to waste, leaned forward. "Okay, Romeo. Let's think logically here. What do we know about this lady? Besides the fact that her smile apparently makes everything else insignificant?"

Arjun sighed, stirring his coffee absentmindedly. "She's... smart. Funny. She likes books. We talked about that book stall at the corner of the street."

"Aha! A clue!" Sameer said, slapping the table. "The bookshop! She might go there again. You should just hang around there, looking totally not creepy, until she shows up."

Arjun rolled his eyes. "Yeah, because that's not weird at all."

"Well, do you have a better idea?"

Before Arjun could reply, a shadow fell across their table. They both looked up to see a waiter holding a small napkin. "Sir, this was left at the counter for you," he said, placing it down.

Arjun frowned, picking up the napkin. Written in neat, looping handwriting was a short message:

You forgot to ask for my number. Lucky for you, I'm not great at waiting for serendipity either. 98xxxxxxxx – Meera.

For a moment, Arjun just stared at the napkin. Sameer leaned over, his eyes widening. "No way. No way! She's even cooler than I thought. She left you her number, dude!"

A grin spread across Arjun's face, wide and unstoppable. "She... left her number."

"Yes, genius, we've established that. Now, are you going to call her, or are we going to frame this napkin and build a shrine around it?"

Arjun's hand hesitated over his phone. "Should I call now? Or would that seem too eager?"

Sameer groaned. "Oh my god. Just call her. She literally left her number for you. What are you waiting for? The stars to align?"

Taking a deep breath, Arjun dialled the number. It rang twice before a familiar, warm voice answered.

"Hello?"

"Hi, Meera. It's Arjun," he said, his voice slightly nervous but steady. "I, uh, just got your note."

She laughed softly, and the sound made his heart skip. "Good. I was starting to think I'd scared you off."

"Scared me off? More like left me speechless," he admitted, a hint of humour in his tone. "Thank you for... this. I wasn't sure if I'd see you again."

"Well, now you don't have to rely on fate," she said. "Though I'm still counting on that accidental bump one of these days."

Arjun chuckled, his nerves easing. "How about we plan the next one? Over coffee?"

"I'd like that," she said, her voice warm. "When?"

"Whenever you're free," he replied quickly, then cringed. "I mean, no rush, of course. Whenever works for you."

Meera laughed again. "How about tomorrow? The same bookshop where we met?"

"Perfect. Tomorrow it is." Thankfully, he had two more days in Jaipur.

They said their goodbyes, and Arjun hung up, his heart feeling lighter than it had in years. He looked up to see Sameer grinning like a proud parent.

"Well, look at you. The man who believes in destiny but finally took matters into his own hands," Sameer teased.

Arjun shook his head, unable to wipe the smile off his face. "You're never going to let me hear the end of this, are you?"

"Never," Sameer said cheerfully. "Now, let's get out of here. You need a new shirt for tomorrow. First impressions, my friend."

As they left the café, Arjun couldn't help but feel that maybe, just maybe, this was the start of something extraordinary.

Their courtship was a whirlwind, filled with stolen moments and shared dreams. Despite the distance, they kept their connection alive through handwritten letters and short calls while Arjun completed his training at the IMA. Those letters became their lifeline, filled with hopes for the future and reassurances of love.

Once Arjun completed his training at IMA, they married in a vibrant ceremony that brought together both families in a joyous celebration.

Meera's father, being a railway officer, initially had reservations about the match due to differences in family backgrounds. He had always envisioned his daughter marrying into a family with a similar social standing, where financial stability and lifestyle expectations aligned. However, despite coming from a farmer's family, Arjun's position as an army officer commanded immense respect and made him a dependable and honourable choice.

The wedding was a colourful blend of traditions, laughter, and a fair share of chaos, courtesy of Arjun's closest friends, Sameer and Raghav. Sameer decided to take charge of the garlands but managed to misplace them right before the exchange. What followed was a dramatic treasure hunt, with relatives and friends scouring every corner of the venue while the bemused priest waited, muttering prayers for patience. Raghav, determined not to be outshone, added his flair for drama by locking himself out of the venue—with the car keys inside. His grand solution? Climbing through a narrow window in his crisp sherwani, which promptly got snagged halfway through, leaving him dangling awkwardly. The photographer, quick on his feet, captured the moment, and it became the highlight of the wedding album. Amidst the hilarity, Arjun and Meera's love shone brightly, as they exchanged vows with tears of joy and promises for a lifetime.

When he put the garland over Meera, Arjun remembered the day he had courageously gone to her house to ask for her hand in marriage. That moment felt like a battle of its own, one where he had to prove not just his love but his worth.

Standing outside Meera's house in his neatly pressed uniform, he had taken a deep breath before knocking on the door.

Meera's mother welcomed him inside with a polite smile, but her father, Mr. Sharma, remained seated, his expression serious. As Arjun sat across from him, the weight of the moment settled in.

Mr. Sharma spoke first, his voice measured. "I know why you're here. Meera has told us about you. But tell me, why do you think you are the right man for my daughter?"

Arjun straightened his posture. "Sir, I understand your concerns. Meera comes from a well-settled family, and I belong to a farming household. But my values, my discipline, and my love for her will always be my priority. I have dedicated my life to serving the country, and I will dedicate my life to keeping her happy and secure."

Mr. Sharma leaned back, crossing his arms. "A stable family background matters. You know how society thinks. People will talk."

Arjun met his gaze steadily. "Sir, I have never been concerned about what society thinks. My father is a farmer, and I am proud of my roots. He taught me the value of hard work and honesty, and today, I stand on my own merit. I may not come from wealth, but I can promise you that Meera will always have respect, security, and love in my home."

There was a long silence. Meera's mother glanced at her husband, sensing his hesitation. Mr. Sharma studied Arjun before letting out a sigh. "You have conviction, I'll give you that. And you have built a respectable life despite your background."

Arjun nodded. "I don't expect an answer today, Sir. But I want you to know that I am serious about this. I will always take care of Meera, just as you have."

Mr. Sharma's expression softened slightly but remained firm. "Marriage isn't just about promises, Arjun. It's about responsibility. I will take my time to think this over."

Arjun had left that evening without a clear answer, but with a glimmer of hope. However, he was not alone in this fight—Meera had a part to play too. She was determined to marry only him and had made that clear to her parents. More than that, she had reached out to Arjun's parents a few days before he had arrived at her home, speaking to them with warmth and respect when she called. She assured them that she understood their concerns and that she would always honour them as her own.

Arjun had listened to that conversation, a quiet pride swelling in his chest. He knew then that Meera wasn't just fighting for their love—she was embracing everything that came with it, including his family. Now, as he stood beside her, placing the garland over her, he saw her father watching from the front row. The same man who had questioned him that day now had a proud yet emotional look in his eyes.

Arjun smiled to himself. He had won the hardest battle of all—the trust of the man who had raised the woman he loved. And he knew Meera would always stand by his side, just as she had from the very beginning.

Soon after his marriage, Arjun left for his base, having already received his first posting orders—with the Rashtriya Rifles (RR), a counter-insurgency force operating in Jammu and Kashmir.

On the eve of his departure, he and Meera sat together in their small living room, the dim glow of a single lamp casting soft shadows around them. They spoke little, both aware that words could do little to ease the ache of separation. Instead, they held each other, letting their silence speak. Later that night, they made love, unhurried and tender, cherishing the time they had before duty called him away. When morning came, Meera tried to smile, but Arjun could see the worry in her eyes. He cupped her face for a moment, pressing a kiss to her forehead before stepping away, knowing that this goodbye would be the first of many.

***

[1]'There is a mystery on your face.'

CHAPTER FOUR

BECOMING A FATHER

It was a little more than a month into his posting when Meera told Arjun she was pregnant. The news came to him over a patchy phone call, her voice breaking through the static with a mix of excitement and nervousness. For a moment, Arjun couldn't speak. The weight of her words settled over him, bringing a rush of emotions he hadn't expected. Joy, disbelief, and a deep longing to be by her side all swelled within him at once.

"Are you sure?" he finally managed, his voice quieter than he intended.

Meera laughed, a soft, happy sound. "I took the test twice, just to be sure."

Arjun leaned against the cold metal of the bunker wall, closing his eyes as he pictured her—probably sitting on their bed, one hand resting on her belly, even though there was nothing to show yet. He imagined the way her face must have lit up when she saw the result, the way she must have wished he were there to hold her.

"I wish I could see you right now," he said, rubbing a hand over his face.

"Me too," she whispered. "You know, you are the first to know... Before anyone else."

The reality of it sank in slowly. He was going to be a father. A rush of pride filled his chest, followed by a deep pang of longing. He wanted to be home, to see the first signs of change in her, to watch over her, to share every small moment leading up to the arrival of their child. But he was miles away, bound by duty.

"How are you feeling?" he asked, concern creeping into his voice.

Meera sighed, running a hand over her stomach. "A little tired. And I keep getting nauseous in the mornings. But I'm okay." She smiled a bit, remembering the funny moments her nausea had caused over the past few days. Just last morning, she had rushed to the sink after catching a whiff of her favourite masala tea with extra cardomom, only to laugh at herself afterward. She had spent days wondering if something was wrong with her stomach, blaming everything from stale food to stress, until the truth had dawned on her. Now, even with the discomfort, there was a quiet happiness settling in—something new, something life-changing.

Arjun frowned. "Are you eating properly? Taking rest?"

"Yes, Arjun. Stop worrying," she said, a smile in her voice, then added, I will call Maa over after I tell them. I found out only today."

She had planned to shift to her home for the next few months. Her parents would have to pause their travels for a while—something they cherished. Usually, they were off on some holiday, exploring a new destination, enjoying their retired life. Meera hoped they wouldn't complain too much about staying back. She knew they would be thrilled about the baby, but the thought of being tied down might make them a little restless.

"I will call your parents today too and tell them," she added, twirling the hem of her dupatta between her fingers.

Arjun smiled to himself. He could imagine her sitting cross-legged on their bed, lost in thought, already worrying about how everyone would react. "They'll all be happy, Meera. You know that," he reassured her.

"I know," she sighed. "I just... I wish you were here."

The longing in her voice made his chest tighten. He wished he could be there too, holding her hand when she broke the news to their families, watching their mothers fuss over her, seeing the first signs of change in her. Instead, he was here, miles away, in a cold bunker surrounded by the quiet hum of duty.

"I'll come as soon as I can," he promised again, wishing he had more control over his leave.

Meera nodded, even though he couldn't see her. "Take care of yourself, Arjun. That's all I want right now."

"You too," he murmured, feeling the ache of distance settle in.

As the call ended, Meera leaned back against the bed's headboard, resting a protective hand over her stomach. A soft smile played on her lips. Their baby. Their little world growing within her.

Arjun, on the other hand, sat in silence, staring at the phone. The mountains stretched outside, the night quiet except for the occasional rustle of wind against the roofs. He exhaled, running a hand through his hair. Life had changed in an instant. He was still a soldier, but now, he was something more—a father-to-be.

In the days that followed he wanted to be by her side every single day. See the changes in her, to share in her cravings, to be the one who brought her fresh fruit in the mornings and massage her feet when they ached at night. But he could not go.

He had promised her, time and again, that he would try. But his leave was not in his control. There was no war, no national emergency, but since he was with the RR, his inability to take leave despite the absence of full-scale conflict made perfect sense. The RR was not like a regular Army battalion—it was a force that lived and breathed counter-insurgency. In Jammu and Kashmir, peace was a fragile illusion, one that could shatter at the sound of a single gunshot. His unit was always on alert, always prepared for the unexpected.

Maybe if things had been quieter, if his sector hadn't seen movement across the border, if there weren't whispers of a new infiltration route, he could have left. But more often than not intelligence sent warnings of militant activity in the nearby hills. The roads had to be constantly watched, the forests were restless, and his unit was perpetually on high alert. Leave requests were buried under stacks of classified reports.

He knew that if he had pushed harder, there were other reasons why he would not be able to walk away. The rotation schedule was unpredictable—until a replacement came, he would be the one holding the line; and a replacement's coming took time. Command decisions took time, and paperwork moved at its own pace, often too slow for the urgency of real life. And beyond all this, it was duty that held him back.

The best he managed in Meera's 37-week pregnancy had been a short three-day vacation when her first trimester was ending,and even that had felt like a stolen moment rather than a choice. He had barely settled into the rhythm of their togetherness before he had to leave again. Those three days had been all he had of her pregnancy in person—just enough time to notice how her face had begun to glow, how her laughter was softer, how she carried herself differently now.

The weeks turned into months, each one slipped by with nothing but phone calls to bridge the distance. He imagined being there for every milestone—feeling the first flutter of movement, watching the curve of her belly grow, witnessing the way her expressions shifted with every new sensation of carrying life inside her. But it remained imagination. His attempts to take more leave had been met with rejections.

His immediate supervisor had sighed sympathetically but ultimately said, "We need you here, you know how it is."

It took him till nearly the end of Meera's pregnancy to finally get leave. His baby was coming. His father-in-law had called to give him the update from the doctor. He had to be with Meera. Nothing would stop him. When he reached home, he barely took a moment to breathe before going to her. She was sitting on the bed, one hand resting on her stomach, her face lighting up when she saw him.

"You're here," she whispered.

"I'm here," he said, and this time, he wasn't making a promise he could not keep.

He held her hand properly for the first time in months, kissed her fingers, and then placed his palm on her bulging tummy. The baby kicked against his hand, and the sensation sent a jolt of emotion through him.

"I wanted you here," she said softly. "Every day, I wished you were here. But I also knew you were trying."

He cupped her face, his thumb brushing against her cheek. "I should have tried harder."

Meera opened her mouth to reply, but a sudden, sharp pain shot through her abdomen. She gasped, gripping his hand as her body tensed.

"Meera?" His voice was thick with concern.

She inhaled shakily. "I think... I think it's time."

Arjun blinked, his heart skipping a beat. "Already? But I just walked in!"

Despite the sharp pain twisting through her, Meera let out a breathless laugh. "Guess the baby couldn't wait for a grand reunion." She clutched his hand tightly as another contraction rippled through her body, her laughter quickly turning into a low groan.

Arjun's panic flared. "Okay, okay—deep breaths. Like we practiced, right?"

She shot him a wry look between clenched teeth. "We practiced? You weren't there for the classes, remember?"

Guilt flashed across his face, but he pushed it aside. "Then I'll improvise." He slid his arm around her shoulders, supporting her as he called out, "Ma! Come quickly!"

His mother-in-law rushed in, her face tightening with understanding the moment she saw Meera doubled over.

"It's happening," Arjun said, his voice strained.

His father-in-law grabbed the car keys and urged, "Call Arjun's parents—tell them to get to Jaipur as soon as possible," while his wife helped Meera toward the door.

Meera's grip on Arjun's hand tightened with another contraction. She gasped, leaning into him.

"I've got you," he whispered, guiding her carefully.

They made it to the car, and Arjun helped her into the backseat before sliding in beside her. His father-in-law started the engine, speeding through the quiet streets, while his mother-in-law stayed on the phone, ensuring that everyone was informed.

Meera's breaths came in uneven bursts as she squeezed his hand with surprising strength. "You're not passing out on me, are you?" she teased through the pain, her forehead damp with sweat.

Arjun let out a shaky chuckle. "Are you kidding? I'm too scared to even blink."

She exhaled a trembling laugh, then winced as another contraction hit.

He wrapped an arm around her, rubbing slow circles on her back. "I'm not going anywhere," he murmured. "Not this time."

Her fingers clutched his shirt, and as the pain ebbed slightly, she looked up at him, her eyes filled with emotion. "Then let's go meet our baby."

Meera and Arjun's life grew tenfold with the birth of their son, Aarav. The night Aarav came into the world was etched into Arjun's memory like a vivid painting—a swirl of emotions, fear, hope, and love, all mingling into one.

He peeked into the delivery room every chance he got, his heart aching at the sight of Meera's determined yet exhausted face.

"She's strong", the nurse reassured him, but the strain in her voice didn't escape him.

Arjun nodded, forcing a smile, but his mind raced. What if something went wrong? He couldn't imagine life without Meera, and now, their child too.

Sameer's voice crackled through the phone when Arjun called him for reassurance. "Calm down, buddy," Sameer said, trying to inject humour. "It's not a battlefield, it's a hospital. Meera's a fighter, and the baby's probably already plotting how to keep you awake all night."

Arjun chuckled despite himself but couldn't shake the worry. Hours ticked by, each second dragging like an eternity. Finally, the doctor emerged with a smile that Arjun clung to like a lifeline.

"Congratulations," she said. "You have a healthy baby boy.'

For a moment, Arjun's knees felt weak. He stepped into the room, his eyes immediately finding Meera. She looked tired but radiant, cradling a tiny bundle wrapped in soft blue. "Arjun," she whispered, her voice hoarse but filled with joy. "Meet Aarav."

Arjun approached slowly as if the gravity of the moment needed to be absorbed step by step. He knelt beside Meera, his eyes misty.

"He's so small," he murmured, his fingers gently brushing Aarav's cheek.

The baby stirred, letting out a soft whimper that made Arjun's heart swell. Both sets of grandparents gathered around, their joy evident as they welcomed the new baby.

Meera smiled weakly. "He's ours."

"He's perfect," Arjun whispered, his voice breaking. He looked at Meera, his expression a mix of gratitude and awe. "You're amazing, you know that? I was terrified out there, and here you were, bringing him into the world like a warrior."

Meera laughed softly, wincing slightly. "A warrior who needs a lot of rest."

Arjun kissed her forehead. "Rest... I've got this."

That night, as he held Aarav for the first time, Arjun felt his world shift. The baby's tiny fingers curled around his own, anchoring him in a way he'd never felt before. At that moment, fatherhood became not just a responsibility but a privilege he was eager to embrace. With Meera by his side and Aarav in his arms, Arjun knew his life had found a new purpose, one filled with love and endless possibilities.

***

CHAPTER FIVE

THE CALL

In the early days of May 1999, whispers of conflict in Kargil had begun to ripple through to his unit. The winds carried murmurs of unusual movements near the Line of Control, but nothing was certain yet. Initial reports were vague, almost hesitant, as if the gravity of the situation had not yet settled into the minds of those receiving them. Soldiers gathered in small groups, discussing the news over steel cups of steaming tea, their voices tinged with curiosity and scepticism.

The base, usually abuzz with the predictable rhythm of drills and daily duties, felt different. There was an unspoken tension in the air, a sense of anticipation that neither the officers nor the men could entirely shake off. Some dismissed the reports as another border skirmish, the kind that flared up occasionally and faded just as quickly. Others, particularly the more experienced soldiers, sensed something more. The mountains of Kargil were not known for such disruptions, and the idea of infiltration in such harsh terrain was unsettling.

Late at night, radio transmissions crackled with updates, but they were frustratingly inconclusive. Orders had not yet come in, but the waiting itself felt like a mission. Arjun found himself lying on his cot, staring at the canvas roof of his tent, his mind racing through possibilities. Would they be deployed? Was this going to be another brief flare-up, or something much bigger? The uncertainty gnawed at him, but he knew one thing for sure—something was shifting, and it would soon demand their presence on the battlefield.

"It's just another routine skirmish," one soldier muttered dismissively, stretching out his legs after a long day.

"You think so?" Sameer questioned. "Reports are saying they're settling in high-altitude positions. That's not just an infiltration—it's an occupation."

Raghav added, "It doesn't feel right. If they're taking those peaks, it's not just a minor incursion. We could be looking at something much bigger."

Arjun remained quiet, his thoughts already drifting homeward. He had managed to get a week's leave sanctioned, a rare respite amid the tension. It had been long pending. Yet, even as he allowed himself to imagine the serenity of home, the possibility of war loomed over him like an unseen spectre, whispering doubts into the silence. He knew all too well that a single call could cut his leave short, turning a week of rest into mere hours of borrowed time. Still, he longed for those moments of peace, however brief they might be, to remind himself of a world beyond duty, beyond uniform and orders. He had learned to carry the weight of unpredictability, to embrace each homecoming as if it were his last. And so, with a quiet resolve, he tucked away his worries and focused on the journey ahead, determined to make the most of whatever time he had.

During the journey home Arjun found himself reflecting on everything that had transpired. When he finally arrived, the sight of his home filled him with an overwhelming sense of relief. It was all the same, yet everything had changed. Meera stood at the door, her eyes lighting up despite the exhaustion etched into her face. The past few months had been mentally and emotionally draining for her. She had been more than a daughter-in-law to Arjun's parents; she had been a daughter in every sense of the word, tending to them in their final days, offering them solace, and even performing the last rites when the time came. As Arjun met her gaze, he saw the weight of grief she carried, but also the quiet strength that had held their world together in his absence.

Aarav, now a little over one year old, toddled toward him, his tiny hands reaching out. Arjun scooped him up, burying his face in his soft curls, feeling a lump rise in his throat.

"Missed you, little man," he whispered, kissing his son's forehead.

As he held his son close, a wave of bittersweet emotion washed over him. How much had he missed? The first time Aarav had babbled his name, the first wobbly steps, the infectious giggles that once filled the house—moments that should have been his to cherish, now only stories Meera had shared with him over hurried phone calls.

But something else lingered in the child's wide, searching eyes—something Arjun hadn't expected. Aarav had already seen two deaths. He was too young to understand what death meant, but he knew that two familiar faces were suddenly no longer there. His grandfather's chair sat empty, his grandmother's soft voice was gone. He had looked for them, Arjun was sure of it, toddling into rooms where they used to be, waiting for them to return. But they never did. And what did that teach such a young mind? That people could disappear? That love could be here one moment and gone the next? A shadow of fear crossed Arjun's heart. What if, in his tiny world, Aarav had begun to wonder if his father, too, would vanish one day? If love always left?

Arjun tightened his hold, pressing his lips against his son's forehead. "I'm here, little man," he murmured. "I'm not going anywhere."

But as he said it, the weight of life's uncertainty pressed down on him. Would he truly be able to keep that promise?

Meera's words cut his train of thoughts. She was smiling but couldn't hide her worry. "Taking holidays is becoming more difficult, isn't it?" she asked softly, her fingers absentmindedly adjusting Aarav's shirt.

Arjun sighed, nodding. "The situation is tense. There's no telling when I'll be called back."

The news played in the background, reporters speaking urgently about the growing conflict in Kargil. Maps of the rugged terrain flashed on the screen, experts debated strategies, and the word 'war' became impossible to ignore. The weight of duty pressed heavily on Arjun's shoulders, a silent reminder that his time at home was fleeting.

As the evening settled in, Aarav clung to his father, refusing to let go. Arjun held him close, feeling the child's warmth seep into him. But underneath the joy of being home, a quiet sorrow lingered. He felt it. A few months ago, he had lost his father. The old man had not been able to take his wife's sudden passing, the grief and effort taking a toll on his body. Arjun had not been there when his mother had died; he had just joined the RR and had been unable to come.

The regret of not being there for either of his parents during their last days gnawed at him, an unspoken ache that refused to fade. He had always believed there would be more time, that life would allow him one last conversation, one final moment to hold their hands and tell them how much they meant to him. But time had been merciless. His mother had left first, and before he could even process her absence, his father had followed. He had not been there to soothe their fears, to offer them comfort in their final moments, to whisper words of love as they slipped away. Instead, he had received the news from miles away, his world collapsing through a phone call.

The only solace he found was Meera's unwavering presence. She had been there, by his parents' side, ensuring they were not alone in their final moments. When Arjun's mother had fallen ill, Meera had taken a firm decision—she had moved both his parents to their home, refusing to let them suffer in solitude. It had given Aarav precious time with his grandparents, though very little. Even now, he would sometimes look around the house, searching for them, his small face creased with confusion and sadness.

Meera's parents, in contrast, were always on the move. Despite having a house in Jaipur, they rarely stayed there. Her father, a retired railway employee, had spent most of his life traveling, and retirement had done little to curb his wanderlust. "You two are always off somewhere," Meera would say with an exasperated smile whenever they called from yet another destination.

Arjun sat with Meera later that night, after Aarav had finally drifted off to sleep. The house was silent, save for the occasional rustle of leaves outside. Meera looked exhausted, but she still held his hand tightly, as if afraid he would slip away too soon.

"I wish I could be here more," he admitted, tracing patterns on her palm with his thumb.

She shook her head. "I know you have to go. Just promise me you'll be careful."

It was a promise he wanted to make, but deep down, he knew the unpredictability of war. He could only nod, pulling her closer, letting the silence between them say what words could not.

What Meera didn't know was that on the nights when exhaustion finally pulled her into sleep, Arjun would sit in the dim glow of a lamp, writing letters to her and Aarav. Letters filled with the words he might never get to say, memories he hoped they would hold on to, and the love he wished could transcend time. He never knew how he would ensure they found them—because if they did, it would mean he was no longer there. And yet, a part of him believed she would find them when the time was right, tucked away in the bedside drawer, waiting like whispers from a past that never wanted to be forgotten.

But he could not write enough. His week-long leave was cut short. He had barely spent three nights at home when the orders for Operation Vijay came. For the past few days, the family had tried to make the most of Arjun's presence. Meera had cooked all his favourite meals, insisting that he eat to his heart's content. They had spent evenings watching Aarav's antics, laughing together, and cherishing the fleeting moments of normalcy. But the shadow of duty had been ever-present, hanging over them like a silent guest at the dinner table.

When the phone rang that morning, it was as though time had stopped. Arjun answered with a calmness that belied the turmoil within him. The voice on the other end was firm, delivering the orders without room for delay or hesitation. Operation Vijay was now in full swing, and his unit was being mobilised to reinforce the troops already engaged in the conflict. As he hung up, a heavy silence filled the room. Aarav, too young to understand, continued to play, his laughter echoing in the stillness.

Arjun turned to Meera, his heart sinking as he met her steady look. She had always been his anchor, the one who kept him grounded when the weight of his responsibilities threatened to overwhelm him. This time was no different.

Without a trace of fear or doubt, she simply nodded and said, "We'll be waiting for you. Always."

Her words were simple, but they carried a strength that bolstered him. She understood the life they had chosen together, the sacrifices it demanded, and the courage it required.

When Arjun left for the operation, the mood sombre yet resolute. Meera helped him pack his duffel bag, slipping a small note into one of the pockets. As he kissed Aarav goodbye, the little boy giggled, oblivious to the gravity of the moment.

Arjun hugged Meera tightly, whispering, "I'll come back to you."

She nodded, her voice steady as she said, "I know you will."

But before returning to his base, there was one last duty Arjun had to fulfil—he had to visit his roots. He had not been there for his parents in their final days, but he could not leave without returning to the place where his story had begun.

The journey from Jaipur to Tonk was a passage through time itself. The city's chaos faded into quieter roads lined with kachori stalls and tea vendors, the scent of spices lingering in the warm air. As the bus rumbled past mustard fields and lone banyan trees, memories surfaced—his childhood races through these very fields, his mother's laughter echoing in the breeze. From Tonk, the roads grew narrower, dust curling up in swirls as the vehicle trudged towards Bhairavgarh. The village emerged like an old, forgotten song—mud-walled houses, temple bells ringing in the distance, the air thick with the scent of earth and familiarity.

Stepping onto the soil of his ancestors, Arjun felt the weight of his absence press upon him. Everything had changed, yet nothing had. The summer sun dipped low over Bhairavgarh, casting golden hues over the sprawling fields that had sustained the Rathore family. Lieutenant Arjun Rathore stood before the weathered stone house that had once been his sanctuary. The ancestral home, now silent, bore the weight of memories—of laughter, struggle, and love. This would be his final visit before reporting for Operation Vijay.

***

CHAPTER SIX

THE JOURNEY TO THE FRONTLINE

As the bus to Delhi rumbled forward, Bhairavgarh faded into the dusty horizon, but its echoes lingered within him. Faces flashed through his mind—his parents, Meera, little Aarav, their expressions frozen in time. His uncle's face surfaced too, another presence lost to the years. People left, and yet they didn't. Their voices, their laughter, their absence—they lived on, woven into the fabric of his being. The rhythmic clatter of the wheels against the worn road blurred the world outside, drawing him deeper into the life he was leaving behind and the duty that awaited him.

As a boy, he had watched soldiers pass through the village, their uniforms crisp, their presence commanding, their stories etched with sacrifice. He had idolized them, dreamt of a life marked by honour. And now, that boy had become one of them. Soon, he would be with his unit—the Rashtriya Rifles—marching toward Kargil, a key force under the 15 Corps, later known as the White Knight Corps. Their mission was clear: to reclaim the heights lost in the Pakistani intrusion. As the bus pressed on, so did the weight of what lay ahead.

In Delhi, at the bustling railway station, Arjun stood amidst the sea of travellers, his duffel bag slung over his shoulder. As he waited for his unit to arrive, the weight of his duty settled in—this was no ordinary journey; it was one that could change everything.

As the train crossed vast plains, Arjun's thoughts oscillated between the past and the uncertain future. The green fields zipped past the window, their serenity a stark contrast to the chaos awaiting him in the mountains. He stared at the expanse, trying to absorb the tranquillity of the moment, knowing full well that it might be the last he would witness for a long time. The rhythmic clatter of the train tracks seemed almost like a heartbeat, steady but ominous, as if echoing the pulse of the journey that lay ahead—a journey that would test every ounce of his endurance and resolve.

The togetherness within the train compartment was palpable, yet subdued. Laughter and conversations broke out occasionally, but they were tinged with an underlying tension. Each soldier carried his thoughts, his worries, and his unspoken fears. Arjun sat by the window, the rhythmic clatter of the train wheels blending with the murmur of voices. His look shifted between the rapidly changing scenery and his comrades, his mind a swirl of reflections.

In the midst of it all, Sameer pulled out a harmonica from his pocket. He began to play a lively tune, the notes rising above the hum of the train. The melody brought a moment of levity, and soon, a few voices joined in, singing an old folk song that echoed memories of home. Even Arjun, lost in his thoughts, found himself smiling at the sight of Sameer's earnest performance.

"You could charm the enemy into surrendering with that harmonica!" A soldier quipped, drawing laughter from the group.

As the laughter settled, Raghav, who had been quietly observing the scene, leaned toward Arjun. "You remember that night at the academy?" he began, a mischievous glint in his eye.

Arjun's brow furrowed in mock confusion. "Which one, Raghav? There were too many disasters to count."

Raghav grinned, ignoring the jab. "The one where you thought climbing the mess roof to retrieve your cadet cap was a good idea."

The memory clicked, and Arjun groaned, rubbing his temple as laughter bubbled up. "I didn't think it through, did I?"

"You? Think through? Never!" Raghav teased. "Sameer and I told you to let it go, but no, you had to play the hero. And what happened? You got stuck halfway, and we had to form a human chain to pull you down before the drill sergeant caught us!"

The group erupted into laughter again, even Sameer pausing his harmonica to chuckle. "Don't forget the part where he nearly took us all down with him. My shoulder was sore for a week!" Sameer added, feigning indignation.

Arjun threw up his hands in mock surrender. "Alright, alright. I admit it wasn't my finest hour. But at least I didn't leave my rifle behind during the drill like Raghav!"

The tables turned, and the banter continued.

As the laughter subsided, another soldier decided to lighten the mood further. He began to recount a tale of his last visit home, embellishing it with outrageous details about a supposed encounter with a mischievous monkey that had stolen his mother's prized mangoes. His animated storytelling, complete with exaggerated gestures, had the compartment in fits of laughter, the tension momentarily forgotten.

The train carried them forward, but for that brief moment, they were back at the academy—carefree cadets with dreams as big as the sky. As the harmonica resumed its melody, Arjun leaned back, a faint smile lingering.

When the train made a brief stop at a small station, the soldiers disembarked to stretch their legs. A vendor selling piping hot tea approached, and one of them, ever the joker, decided to barter one of his rations for an extra cup.

The vendor, amused by the audacity, handed over the tea with a laugh. "Yeh humari taraf se aapko. Baas, humein yeh jung jitado."[1]

Arjun wondered how much the common man truly understood about the realities of war. They saw the headlines, the fiery debates on television, and the patriotic songs that played on the radio, but did they grasp the weight of it all? Did they feel the biting cold of the mountains or hear the deafening silence that followed a soldier's last breath? The war wasn't just a clash of armies; it was a story of two nations that had once been one. The same language, the same culture, the same food—and yet, now divided by borders, by politics, by history.

This divide was visible everywhere, from the cricket field to the rugged terrains of the Himalayas. Every match between India and Pakistan carried the weight of a war in itself, with millions glued to their screens, cheering for their team as if the fate of their nation depended on it. And now, here they were, fighting not for trophies but for territory, for lives, for peace. Arjun couldn't help but think about the people on the other side—farmers, shopkeepers, teachers—men who might have been his neighbours in another lifetime, now his enemies. What did they feel? Did they pray for their soldiers the same way Indian families prayed for theirs?

Back on the train, it was quieter now; the hum of the wheels was a steady backdrop to the soldiers' unspoken thoughts. Arjun knew that the others, like him, were grappling with the fragility of promises made to loved ones. He thought of Meera and felt achingly distant. War, he knew, was an unpredictable force, one that cared nothing for personal stories, dreams, or the bonds that tied people to each other. It was an unfeeling entity, capable of shattering lives in an instant and reducing years of love and aspirations to fragments of memory. Arjun had seen it before in the eyes of veterans—men who returned home with medals but without the light in their eyes, their losses etched deeper than their triumphs. He wondered if he would one day be one of them, carrying the weight of lives lost, both friend and foe. Yet, amidst this sobering reflection, he clung to the hope that his training and his will to return would prevail.

Looking around the compartment, he saw similar emotions flickering in the faces of his comrades—determination, fear, and a quiet resolve. It was in this shared understanding that they found solidarity, a bond forged not just in duty but in the acknowledgement of the risks they faced.

"War may be merciless," Arjun thought, "but it was their unwavering commitment to protect all that they held dear that gave their journey meaning."

In the stillness of the train, he closed his eyes, summoning strength from the promise he made to himself: to fight with honour, to protect those who depended on him, and to hold on to the hope of a tomorrow where he could keep his word.

He tried to shake off the heaviness, focusing instead on the mission that awaited him. His unit was known for its exceptional counterinsurgency operations and its role in defending the nation's sovereignty. Being a part of it was both an honour and a burden, especially as they were now tasked with reclaiming the strategic heights seized during the Kargil conflict.

As the train neared Jammu, the landscape began to change dramatically. The sprawling plains gradually gave way to undulating hills. By the time the soldiers disembarked, the air had turned cooler, carrying with it the first whispers of the mountains. Military trucks were waiting to transport them further into the heart of Jammu and Kashmir.

The sight of these military trucks filled Arjun with a mix of resolve and unease. Their sturdy frames, weathered by countless journeys, seemed to embody the resilience required for the path ahead. As he climbed aboard, the cold metal of the truck's sides felt both grounding and foreboding, a stark reminder of the unforgiving terrain they were about to traverse. Arjun couldn't help but think of the countless soldiers these vehicles had carried before him—each with their own hopes, fears, and destinies. The trucks seemed like silent witnesses to the weight of their mission, yet steadfast in their purpose, much like the soldiers they ferried.

The convoy rumbled through the outskirts of towns, climbing steadily into more rugged terrain. The air grew thinner as the landscape shifted, the once vibrant vegetation giving way to rugged, windswept rocks. Jagged peaks pierced the sky, their sharp outlines etched against the fading light, casting long, eerie shadows over the jagged terrain. The ground beneath was uneven, with loose stones and rocky outcrops that made every step a challenge. The faint rustling of the wind through the sparse, hardy shrubs was the only sound that accompanied their journey, as the vast emptiness of the mountain range seemed to swallow every other noise. A sense of solitude settled in, the silence broken only by the occasional gust of wind. The path ahead seemed endless, yet every step felt like an invitation to uncover the mysteries that lay beyond. The mountains, stoic and ancient, held secrets in their depths, their towering presence both a challenge and a beckoning to those daring enough to explore. Arjun was struck by how quickly the familiar gave way to the foreign. Each passing mile felt like a step into another world, one defined by isolation and stark beauty.

The roads grew narrower and more treacherous as they climbed higher. Jagged rock faces jutted out ominously, and the convoy moved cautiously, the trucks often halting at precarious bends. The drivers navigated with precision, but the steep inclines and sharp turns tested even the most experienced among them. The soldiers remained alert, aware that the terrain itself was an adversary. Arjun watched as the world outside the truck's window became increasingly desolate. The mountains were imposing, their peaks capped with snow that glistened under the weak sunlight.

The journey was an ordeal. The biting cold seeped through their uniforms, and the thin air made every breath a conscious effort. The higher they climbed, the more the enormity of the terrain bore down on them. Each soldier coped in his own way—some closed their eyes, retreating into their thoughts, while others exchanged quiet words of encouragement. Arjun found himself contemplating the unpredictability of the mission ahead. War was not just about strategy and firepower; it was about endurance and adaptability. The enemy was not only the adversary hiding in the mountains but also the environment itself. The soldiers' resilience would be tested at every step, from navigating the treacherous passes to surviving the harsh climate.

As the convoy advanced, they passed through small villages nestled in the valleys, their humble dwellings dotting the landscape like a peaceful oasis amid the harshness of the mountains. The sight of children playing in the dirt, their laughter echoing through the narrow streets, and women tending to livestock, weaving through the dust with baskets of food, brought a fleeting sense of normalcy. It was a world far removed from the towering peaks and barren wilderness surrounding them. These simple yet enduring acts of daily life were a poignant reminder of the lives they were protecting, the lives that depended on the safety and stability the convoy sought to ensure. The smoke rising from chimneys added a warm contrast to the cold, unyielding terrain, a symbol of hope in an otherwise unforgiving world. Yet, these moments of connection were fleeting, quickly replaced by the starkness of the wilderness. The roads continued to climb, winding through narrow passes where landslides were a constant threat. The trucks groaned under the strain of their heavy loads, their engines labouring against the inclines. At times, the convoy would stop at precarious points, allowing the soldiers to stretch their legs. The silence of the mountains was profound, broken only by the occasional sound of distant avalanches or the roar of a fighter jet overhead.

Arjun's mind often wandered back to the unpredictability of war. Reclaiming the heights would be no easy feat. He felt a deep sense of pride knowing that he was part of such a storied unit. The 15 Corps was a formidable force responsible for safeguarding the Line of Control. Their mission was not just about reclaiming territory; it was about restoring India's honour and securing its borders against future incursions.

The soldiers sang songs to lighten the mood, yet, beneath the friendship lay a shared understanding of the stakes. Every soldier knew someone who had not returned from a mission. As night fell, the convoy stopped at a temporary base camp, the soldiers weary but resolute. They disembarked, stretching their stiff limbs and huddling around small fires for warmth, the crackling flames offering both comfort and companionship. The air was thick with the scent of freshly cooked food—simple but nourishing stews of rice and lentils, flatbreads roasted on open flames, and the occasional splash of spiced tea. As they ate, the soldiers shared tales from home, tales of distant relatives, of childhood memories, and of the lives they left behind. Laughter mixed with the deep murmur of quiet conversations, and the rhythm of songs—some old, some improvised—began to fill the air. The melodies, though rough and unpolished, carried a sense of unity, a reminder that even in the heart of the wilderness, they were not alone.

In the middle of the meal, Raghav began telling a tale that quickly became the highlight of the night. "So, there I was," he said, wiping his mouth with the back of his hand, "sitting at the family dinner table, watching my grandmother's prized goat stew being served. But the goat, it wasn't quite as tender as she promised!" The others leaned in, intrigued. "Turns out, my grandmother had mistaken a neighbour's goat for her own, and not just any goat—one that had been chewing on thorns for weeks! We all took a bite, and it was like eating leather!" He mimicked chewing intensely, and the camp erupted in laughter. "Grandma was so proud of the stew, but every time we tried to chew, we'd just smile and nod. We ended up pretending it was the best meal ever, though we could barely swallow a bite!"

The story lightened the mood, and the soldiers laughed heartily, some of them joking about the toughness of their own rations. One soldier, after unwrapping his meal packet, stared at it for a moment with a perplexed expression. He held up a piece of what was supposed to be bread, but it looked more like a brick. With a dramatic sigh, he attempted to break it in half, but the bread didn't budge. After several unsuccessful attempts, he slapped it against his knee in frustration, only for it to bounce back up like a rubber ball. The soldiers who were watching erupted in laughter, marvelling at how the so-called bread had managed to survive the journey. It was clear that their meals were designed to withstand anything, but the soldiers couldn't help but wonder if they might be better suited for building houses rather than feeding hungry men.

Another pulled out a packet of dehydrated soup, which, when rehydrated, was supposed to resemble a hearty meal. He carefully followed the instructions, adding water and stirring it with the provided spoon. However, when he took his first sip, his face contorted into a look of shock. The soup had no flavour, and the texture was like thin wallpaper paste. He tried to hide his disappointment, but the others quickly caught on. Laughter followed, as the soldier, holding up the bowl, muttered that the soup tasted more like the sweat of a thousand soldiers than anything remotely edible. Despite their grumbling, they all took turns taking a sip, each making exaggerated faces at the taste. The shared misery over their rations turned into a moment of amusement and a reminder that they were all in the same boat. In these moments, albeit temporarily, under the stars, the harsh realities of their journey seemed to fade into the background as the warmth of their bond filled the air.

Arjun beheld at the stars above, feeling both humbled and invigorated. The enormity of the universe seemed to dwarf their struggles, yet it also reminded him of the larger purpose they served. Protecting their nation's sovereignty was not just a duty; it was a calling. The unpredictability of war was a constant shadow, but it was one they had all learned to live with. In these moments, around the fire and under the vast canopy of stars, the weight of their mission felt both heavy and hopeful, as if the universe itself nodded in silent approval of their sacrifice.

The journey resumed at dawn, the trucks inching closer to their destination. The terrain grew even more unforgiving, with snow-covered passes and icy winds that bit through their layers. Arjun could feel the anticipation building among the soldiers. They were nearing Kargil, where the mission would truly begin. The thought of engaging in battle both exhilarated and sobered him. He knew the odds were steep, but he also knew that they had the training and the resolve to overcome them.

When the convoy approached the conflict zone, the soldiers were briefed on the stakes. Arjun's face was a mask of calm determination as his thoughts churned with the enormity of the task ahead. The jagged peaks loomed in the distance, cloaked in an eerie silence that seemed to echo the weight of the mission.

The commanding officer stepped into the makeshift briefing room, a rugged tent pitched against the cold, barren landscape. A map of the Dras sector lay pinned on a board, illuminated by a dim lantern. The officer wasted no time, his voice firm yet empathetic.

"Our next target is Tololing," he began, pointing to the map with his gloved hand. "This peak is one of the most strategically significant positions occupied by the enemy. From here, they have a direct line of sight over the Srinagar-Leh highway. If we don't reclaim it, our supply lines remain vulnerable, and the enemy holds the upper hand."

Arjun leaned forward, studying the map. Tololing's sharp inclines and rugged terrain stood out starkly, and he could already feel the weight of the challenge settling in his chest. These battles would become some of the most fiercely contested in Indian military history. The terrain mirrored the stakes: sharp inclines, icy pathways, and an unrelenting wind that cut through their uniforms. Every step forward demanded resolve, both physical and mental.

The officer continued, his voice growing graver. "The enemy is heavily entrenched. They've fortified their positions with bunkers and machine-gun nests. Their vantage point gives them a deadly advantage—they'll see us coming long before we can get close. The climb is steep, the air is thin, and the temperature will drop to sub-zero levels at night. This mission will not be easy, but it is necessary."

The room fell silent as the weight of the mission sank in. For a moment, all that could be heard was the wind howling outside the tent. Arjun's look drifted to his comrades, their faces lit with a mix of determination and trepidation.

The officer's tone softened slightly. "You're not just soldiers. You're the hope of a nation watching and waiting. Reclaiming Tololing is not just a tactical necessity—it's a message. A message that no one can take what is ours."

The briefing concluded, but Arjun's mind lingered on the details. He visualised the steep climb, the icy winds cutting through their gear, and the enemy watching from above, waiting to strike. He felt the familiar churn of emotions—a mix of fear, resolve, and an unshakable sense of duty. Dras had, indeed, transformed from a quiet, remote valley into a theatre of war. The enemy's occupation of peaks like Tololing had turned this tranquil land into a zone of relentless artillery and gunfire, with its strategic vantage points threatening. Some locals had evacuated but had left behind traces of their lives—prayer flags fluttering in the wind and small shrines dotting the landscape. Would they ever return to their homes?

His mind wandered to the valley's tranquil summers when wildflowers like vivid blue poppies and the occasional edelweiss adorned the landscape. He wondered when blooms would return, and if the snow leopards and Himalayan ibex would once again roam these heights freely. The thought of Dras reclaiming its peace, transforming into a haven where travellers come not for war memorials but to marvel at its untouched beauty and meet its warm, resilient people, filled him with a wistful longing.

Meera had once recited to him the poignant lines from John McCrae's *In Flanders Fields*, "In Flanders fields, the poppies blow; Between the crosses, row on row..." The memory of her voice brought a soft smile to his lips. He recalled how they had postponed their honeymoon, and the absurdity of suggesting Dras as a destination made him chuckle silently. His thoughts shifted rapidly—from the beauty of the valley, to Meera's laughter, to the camaraderie with his fellow soldiers, to war, guns, death.... Each thought unrelated and yet intertwined. Arjun made a silent promise that life and beauty would return, just as the poppies had once bloomed in Flanders fields.

As he stepped out into the cold night air, Arjun paused to take in the silhouette of the looming peaks against the starry sky. Tololing was out there, its presence imposing and unyielding. He thought of his family back home and what his mother used to tell him during his growing-up years, "Apna farz nibhana, beta, chahe kuch bhi ho jaye."[2]

He heard a sound and turned to see Raghav. Their eyes met, and for a brief moment, the harsh world around them faded. They had trained together, endured countless hardships, and forged a bond stronger than the mountains themselves. Raghav, always the optimist, met Arjun's look with a reassuring grin. "It's tough, but we've trained for this. We'll see it through."

Arjun nodded, drawing strength from his friend's quiet confidence.

The night continued, the biting cold seeping into every inch of their gear as they rested in tense silence. The following morning, the first light of dawn revealed the daunting task ahead. The next day, preparations began in earnest. They were about to step into one of the fiercest battles of their lives, but they would do so together, with courage in their hearts and the weight of a nation's hopes on their shoulders. The soldiers checked their gear, studied the routes, and shared quiet moments of fellowship.

He told himself, "We'll make it. Not because it's easy, but because we have no choice. Tololing isn't just a peak—it's our promise to everyone back home that we'll protect what's ours."

The final leg of the journey was on foot. The soldiers, shouldering their weapons and gear, began their ascent. The path was rocky and treacherous, with frost-covered ground and narrow ledges that demanded every ounce of concentration. The air grew thinner, the cold more biting, and every breath felt like an effort. Signs of past battles—charred vehicles, craters, and shattered trees—served as grim reminders of what lay ahead.

Suddenly, a rustling noise ahead halted their progress. The soldiers stopped, instincts honed by combat alerting them to potential danger. Hands tightened on weapons, eyes scanned the dim landscape, and breaths were held in anticipation. The tension was palpable; any unexpected sound in this hostile terrain could signify an enemy presence.

To their surprise, a pika emerged from behind a boulder, its eyes wide with fear. The creature stood on its hind legs, peering at the soldiers with a mix of curiosity and trepidation. Realising the source of the disturbance, the men exchanged relieved glances.

One soldier whispered with a grin, "Looks like we've been ambushed by a furry little scout."

A ripple of subdued laughter spread through the group, easing the tension of the moment.

The pika, perhaps emboldened by the lack of immediate threat, chattered briefly before scurrying away into the rocky terrain. The encounter, though fleeting, provided a moment of levity amidst the gruelling march. With spirits slightly lifted, the soldiers resumed their climb.

Indeed, the fellowship among the soldiers was unspoken but deeply felt. In the harsh and unforgiving terrain of the Kargil heights, where the very landscape seemed to conspire against them, their unity became their strongest asset. The path ahead was treacherous, a narrow, winding route flanked by jagged cliffs that appeared to close in with every step. The soldiers moved as a single entity, each one instinctively aware of the other's movements. There were no words exchanged, but the silent understanding that they were in this together was palpable. A shared glance here, a slight nod there, and the faintest reassuring touch when one soldier stumbled—these small gestures held more weight than any words could convey. Every step was a collective effort, each soldier leaning on the others for strength, unwilling to falter, unwilling to let the team down. The terrain was brutal, a constant reminder of the mountains' indomitable power, but their bond was stronger. It was this unyielding fellowship that gave them the strength to push through, to keep climbing, to keep moving forward.

The final stretch to their destination, however, tested them more than they had anticipated. As they neared the pass leading to Tololing, the terrain became even more punishing. The narrow trail they had been following now dwindled to little more than a sliver of ground, suspended precariously between steep cliffs that seemed to rise endlessly above them. The wind was no longer just a chilling breeze but a fierce, biting force, cutting through their fatigues, scraping the exposed skin of their faces, and carrying with it a bitter cold that seeped into their bones. The ground beneath their boots was uneven, jagged rocks jutting out at odd angles, forcing them to carefully navigate each step. One wrong move could send them tumbling down into the depths below.

Every soldier's body ached, muscles sore from days of climbing, but it was the mental fatigue that was the most taxing. The mountains seemed to stretch on endlessly, the path twisting and turning with no end in sight. Yet, despite the harshness of the terrain, they pressed on. The soldiers moved with a determination borne not only of duty but of an unwavering belief in one another. The mountain was relentless, but so were they. The final stretch was a strenuous test of endurance, but the sight of the ridge ahead, the promise of their goal just within reach, pushed them onward. When they finally reached the heights of Tololing, the situation was more treacherous than they had imagined. The cliffs that surrounded them were even steeper, the rocks more jagged, and the wind even fiercer. The path they had taken now seemed almost like a dream—a distant memory of a time when the terrain had felt just a bit more navigable. But despite the challenges, they stood together, knowing that the terrain, though brutal, was nothing compared to the strength of their unity. They had made it this far together, and together, they would overcome whatever came next.

As the soldiers began to set up positions, the first wave of enemy fire cut through the air like a deadly storm. Machine gun fire erupted from entrenched bunkers above, the relentless chatter of the guns drowning out all other sounds. The enemy's positions were expertly camouflaged, tucked into the natural rock formations and hidden behind layers of earth and debris. Mortars rained down from unseen locations, their shells exploding with deafening force and sending plumes of dust and debris into the air. The explosions created a suffocating blur, blurring visibility and making every move feel like an open invitation to death. The soldiers had no choice but to stay low, crawling and ducking behind whatever meagre cover they could find—rocks, boulders, or the occasional depression in the terrain—anything that would protect them from the hail of incoming fire. The narrow passes and loose terrain, which had once been their challenge, now seemed like traps designed to funnel them directly into the enemy's sights. They were vulnerable on all sides, the enemy's fire coming from well-coordinated positions that allowed no room for error. The soldiers could hear the dull thud of incoming artillery, followed by the sharp whistling sound of mortar rounds as they descended from above, forcing them to scramble for shelter as the ground shook with each explosion.

In the midst of this deadly onslaught, the enemy's tactics became all too clear. They were not only fighting with heavy artillery and machine guns but with a strategic understanding of the battlefield that made the soldiers' positions even more precarious. The enemy's fire was relentless, aimed with precision to pin the soldiers down, keeping them from advancing or retreating. The soldiers could hear the faint crackle of radios in the distance, signalling the enemy's well-coordinated attempts to flank and surround them. It became evident that every move had to be calculated, as the enemy worked to exploit every gap in the soldiers' defence. Above them, the enemy fighters worked in pairs, one providing suppressing fire while the other moved into position to launch grenades or pick off targets with precision rifles. The soldiers quickly realised that the enemy had a clear understanding of the terrain, using it to their advantage, setting up traps, and positioning their forces in ways that made it nearly impossible to predict their next move. The soldiers, however, had no choice but to fight on, knowing that their survival depended on moving in sync, maintaining focus, and constantly adapting to the enemy's evolving tactics. They could not afford to be caught off guard, for every second counted in a fight where the difference between life and death was measured in inches.

Suddenly, there was a sharp crack—a sound that cut through the chaos of the battlefield like a blade. Arjun's heart skipped as he turned towards the source of the sound, only to see Raghav crumple to the ground. His rifle slipped from his grasp as he fell, his face still holding traces of determination that had defined him only moments ago. It was over in an instant, yet the weight of what had happened bore down on Arjun like an eternity. He stiffened for a moment, disbelief gripping him. His mind screamed in denial, but reality stared back, cold and unyielding. Tears didn't come out. Not a drop. He wanted to shout, to reach out and pull Raghav back from the abyss, but no sound escaped his lips. Instead, a raw, hollow ache began to spread through his chest—a pain that was both suffocating and numbing.

The battlefield roared on around him, indifferent to his grief, but for Arjun, time had stopped. All he could do was stare at his fallen friend, his heart breaking under the weight of loss. Raghav had been his brother in every way that mattered. And now, he was gone, his life extinguished by the enemy's precise fire, leaving Arjun with a void that no victory could ever fill.

It was a stark reminder of the fragility of life in war, where death could strike without warning. Arjun felt the weight of the loss, but there was no time for grief. They had a mission to complete, and the mountain would not yield easily.

Each step forward now carried the weight of Raghav's sacrifice. He was gone. Arjun walked on, but his mind kept drifting back to Raghav's sister, the one who had raised him after their parents died in an accident years ago. She was his world, his everything, and now, she would have to be told that her baby brother, the boy she had cared for with such devotion, was no more. Arjun couldn't shake the image of her face when she would hear the news—the pain, the disbelief. He wondered what words could even be used to explain such a loss. Raghav had been her rock, her purpose, and now, lying lifeless in the snow, he would never come back. The Indian Army, as per their protocol, would ensure that Raghav's body was recovered, even in the harshest of conditions. It would be sent back with full military honours, wrapped in the national flag, a final tribute to his service and sacrifice. But what would that mean to his sister? The formalities, the rituals, they could never replace the presence of her brother, her child, the person she had raised with so much love. Arjun knew, that no matter what they did to honour Raghav, the one thing they couldn't give her was the chance to say goodbye. The weight of that thought lingered as they pressed on, moving with calculated precision, relying on flanking tactics and surprise manoeuvres to engage the enemy. The constant barrage of fire from above made every step forward feel like a battle against fate itself. The lack of oxygen at high altitudes made breathing harder, and the cold, sharp winds threatened to chill their very resolve. Yet, the soldiers continued, driven by a shared sense of purpose. Each step was a testament to their strength, their commitment to their nation, and the memory of those who had already given everything.

As the battle intensified, the soldiers of the 15 Corps fought their way through the rugged landscape, inching closer to their objective. The harsh conditions, the constant threat of enemy fire, and the unbearable fatigue were all part of the trials they faced. Yet, despite everything, they pressed on, understanding that the stakes were not just about the land, but about the pride and security of their nation. For Arjun, Tololing had become more than just a peak—it was a symbol of everything he had fought for and everything he had become. The mountain, once an imposing figure in the distance, now felt like a personal adversary, one that demanded everything from him, physically and mentally. Yet, as they neared their goal, Arjun knew that this was only the beginning. The battle was far from over, but with every step forward, they were reclaiming not just the mountain, but their pride, their mission, and their unyielding spirit as soldiers.

***

[1]"This is from me to you. Just make sure to win this battle for us."

[2]"Fulfill your duty, my child, no matter what happens."

CHAPTER SEVEN

POINT 5140

Arjun squinted in the pale moonlight, his breath misting in the frigid air. Point 5140 loomed ahead, an unforgiving fortress of rock and ice that rose sharply from the earth, its jagged edges disappearing into the cold, inky sky. It was the next objective after Tololing, a peak that had already tested their limits. But Point 5140 was different—more challenging, more heavily fortified, and more critical. Somewhere near the summit, the enemy lay entrenched in well-built bunkers, armed with machine guns and mortars, ready to repel any assault. Arjun stood at the base of the peak, his breath visible in the frigid air. He knew the climb would be exhausting, the battle even more so. But there was no turning back. The stakes were not just tactical but deeply personal, as tales of bravery and sacrifice from Tololing still echoed in their minds. Later, all would learn of the haunting aftermath—how the bodies of Pakistani soldiers, unclaimed by their own country, were given dignified last rites by the Indian Army, a solemn act of humanity amidst the bitterness of war. And how, years after the war, the skeletal remains of Indian soldiers who had gone missing during the operation were found in a secluded cave, their personal belongings still intact, telling silent stories of their final moments.

The mission began under a veil of darkness, the soldiers moving in disciplined silence; boots crunching against loose gravel and snow. The climb was steep, the terrain treacherous, each step requiring careful calculation. The icy wind cut through their uniforms, biting into their skin. Every breath was a struggle in the oxygen-starved air, but the soldiers pressed on, their resolve unyielding.

Arjun adjusted his grip on his rifle, its cold steel biting into his gloved hands. The briefing earlier in the day had been clear—this peak was crucial. It was the last stronghold in the sector, and its capture would shift the tide. But plans drawn on paper rarely mirrored the chaos of reality.

"Feels different without Raghav, doesn't it?" Sameer's voice broke the silence, as he walked just behind Arjun.

Arjun glanced over his shoulder, the glow of his headlamp catching Sameer's sombre expression. "It does," he admitted, his voice low, almost drowned by the wind. Not being able to say much. After all, when you lose someone who means a lot to you, words feel empty, and silence speaks louder than anything you can say. Grief has a way of stealing not just joy but also the ability to express it. "Feels like he should be here, cracking some stupid joke to keep us moving."

Sameer managed a weak smile, but it faded as quickly as it appeared. "You remember how he always complained about the cold? Said he'd trade this for a hot desert mission any day."

Arjun nodded, a lump forming in his throat. "Yeah, and he'd still beat us up the hill no matter how much he whined."

They walked in silence for a while, the only sounds were the crunch of snow and the howl of the wind.

Sameer's voice came again, softer this time. "I did not get to sit beside him to even say a proper goodbye."

Arjun placed a hand on his shoulder. "We will. In our own way. When all this is over. For now, we have to finish this. For him."

Sameer nodded, his eyes glistening with unshed tears.

Arjun glanced back and saw exhaustion etched on his comrades' faces, but no one complained. They had faced worse at Tololing. They had survived. Beside him, Naik Baldev climbed with steady determination, his presence an unspoken comfort. The climb was merciless. The higher they went, the more treacherous the path became. Loose rocks skittered underfoot, and icy patches turned every step into a gamble. Occasionally, the silence was broken by the distant crack of gunfire—a reminder that the enemy was watching.

The soldier's footing gave way completely as he stepped on a patch of treacherous loose gravel. His boots slipped out from under him, and with a cry stifled by instinct, he tumbled backwards down the jagged slope. His body struck against sharp rocks, his pack twisting him awkwardly as gravity pulled him relentlessly down. The clatter of his gear and the sickening thuds of his impact against the unforgiving terrain echoed in the cold night air. Dust and shards of stone cascaded alongside him, marking his uncontrolled descent. The others could only watch, helpless, as he slid farther and farther away, the narrow ledge offering no way to intervene. His descent ended abruptly as his body came to rest against a large outcropping, lying motionless in the faint moonlight. The air seemed to hold its breath, the silence now heavier than the noise that had shattered it moments ago.

Arjun froze mid-step, his blood turning to ice as he saw it happen. His heart plummeted, his breath catching in his throat. Arjun's mind screamed at him to react, but his body felt paralysed, rooted to the spot by a sickening sense of déjà vu. He had been just now talking about Raghav, about loss, about absence—and now this? What nonsense was this? How could the universe be so cruel, so utterly chaotic, that it would snatch away another one of them so soon? His grip on his rifle tightened until his knuckles turned white, a futile attempt to ground himself amid the swirling storm of emotions inside.

Without thinking, Arjun began scrambling down the slope after the fallen soldier, his movements desperate, almost reckless. His boots slipped on the loose gravel, sending small rocks cascading down the incline, but he pressed on, his mind clouded with panic. He wouldn't let this happen again. Not like Raghav. Not again.

Suddenly, a firm hand gripped his arm, yanking him back just as his footing gave way. Sameer was there, his face taut with a mix of anger and desperation. "What are you doing, Arjun?" Sameer hissed, his voice sharp but trembling. "Walk. Now. Keep moving!" His words came out like orders, but his eyes betrayed the same raw fear that gripped Arjun.

Before Sameer could say more, the sharp crack of gunfire tore through the air. It transformed the mountain into a battleground, its stillness shattered by the deafening roar of enemy weapons. The tracer rounds streaked through the dark, their fiery arcs briefly illuminating the jagged cliffs and the soldiers scrambling for cover. Arjun's breath came in sharp bursts as he crouched behind a boulder, the cold stone biting into his back. The relentless hammering of machine guns echoed, reverberating off the surrounding peaks and amplifying the chaos. Dust and shards of rock flew with every impact, stinging his exposed skin and filling the air with a sharp, acrid tang. The enemy, perched high above, seemed omnipresent, their firepower raining down with calculated precision. Arjun gripped his rifle tightly, his senses heightened to every sound and movement. Each second felt stretched, the mountain becoming a cruel maze of shadows, noise, and danger as they braced for the next wave.

"Return fire!" their commander yelled, his voice barely audible over the din.

Arjun's unit responded with coordinated fire, their training taking over. A small group moved ahead to flank the enemy, drawing their attention while the rest of the unit advanced cautiously. The incline grew mercilessly steeper, transforming the climb into an excruciating crawl.

The icy ground bit into their gloved hands and knees, its harshness amplified by the numbing cold that seeped through their fatigues. Jagged rocks jutted out from the icy earth, scraping against their skin and tearing at their gear with each forward push. Arjun's world shrank to the immediate sensations around him—the steady crunch of snow beneath his weight, the sharp sting of the frosty air in his lungs, and the rhythmic pounding of his heart, loud in his ears. The mountain loomed ominously above, its rugged surface illuminated faintly by the pale moonlight, while the darkness around them seemed alive with the threat of the unseen enemy. Every inch gained felt like a battle in itself, the unforgiving terrain challenging not just their strength but their very will to persevere.

As they neared the first bunker, the true scale of the challenge became evident. The enemy's fire intensified, relentless and unyielding, cutting through the cold air with deafening precision. Bullets whizzed past, some striking the ground with sharp, metallic pings, while others thudded into rocks, sending fragments flying. Muzzle flashes lit up the darkened ridgeline, revealing glimpses of the enemy's fortified position. Arjun's ears rang from the near-constant volley, the roar of machine guns blending with the occasional, bone-shaking explosion of mortars. He could feel the pressure of each shot in his chest, a grim reminder of their peril. When Nikhil fell, his body crumpling silently to the ground, the weight of the moment hit like a hammer.

Nikhil was a young soldier with an infectious optimism that seemed to defy even the most hostile terrain. Even in this harsh environment, he would often say, "The mountains may be tall, but they've never met someone as stubborn as me." He had spoken of his dreams with a boyish fervour—how he longed to return home to his nephew, who idolised him and hung on his every word. His mother, ever doting, had packed his favourite sweets into his kit, a taste of home to carry him through the journey. Now, that vibrant young man, full of life and promise, lay motionless in the snow, his future extinguished in an instant. The starkness of his stillness was a cruel reminder of the cost of war, the toll it exacted on even the brightest souls. There was no time to grieve. The mission demanded their focus. Arjun clenched his jaw, his grief buried under layers of resolve. He peeked out and fired into the darkness, the muzzle flash illuminating the chaos for a brief second. The firefight was intense, with bullets ricocheting off rocks and mortars exploding around them. The air was thick with the acrid smell of gunpowder.

Soon after, at the commanding officer's signal, the air was pierced by the shrill whistle of grenades hurtling toward their target. The deafening explosions shook the earth, sending plumes of smoke and debris into the air, momentarily silencing the enemy's relentless machine gun fire. The soldiers didn't hesitate; they surged forward like a well-oiled machine, each movement swift and coordinated. The confined space of the bunker amplified every sound—the shouts, the clatter of boots on stone, the sharp reports of rifles and the resounding thud of enemy bodies hitting the ground. Arjun's pulse raced as he moved with precision, his instincts kicking in, each step guided by the exhaustive training that had prepared him for this very moment. His weapon, the INSAS (Indian Small Arms System) rifle, was a constant companion. With its 5.56mm rounds, it was a versatile weapon, capable of both semi-automatic and fully automatic fire, ideal for both close-quarter combat and longer-range engagements. The enemy's fire had been mostly from a heavy MG3 machine gun, its vicious, rapid-fire designed to suppress and overwhelm. But the grenades, fired in perfect unison, had created a brief window of opportunity. Arjun's heart pounded as the team stormed the bunker, a final flurry of activity before the last enemy soldier fell in a heap. The moment of stillness that followed was suffocating, heavy with exhaustion, loss, and the bitter taste of survival. The once-constant barrage of gunfire had subsided, but the weight of what they had just endured lingered in the air, thick and palpable.

They pressed on as the enemy fire slowed, advancing cautiously under the cover of darkness. But the battle wasn't yet done. The summit was still ahead, and the enemy had more bunkers waiting. The climb resumed, the soldiers pushing through their fatigue. Each step was a tribute to the comrades who had fallen along the way. Every inch of progress felt like a small victory. But the closer they got to the summit, the fiercer the resistance became. The Pakistani soldiers were entrenched in well-camouflaged bunkers, their vantage point giving them a deadly advantage.

The tension was palpable. The enemy, aware of the advancing soldiers, unleashed another barrage of gunfire and mortars. Arjun's unit split into two groups, one laying down suppressive fire while the other moved in for the assault. The chaos of battle was overwhelming, but amidst it, there was a clarity of purpose. The final moments were a blur of action and emotion. Arjun found himself leading the charge alongside Havildar Sukhram. They climbed the last stretch under relentless fire, every muscle in their bodies screaming in protest. The summit seemed impossibly far, but they pressed on, driven by a shared resolve.

Then it happened. A sharp crack echoed through the air, followed by a sickening thud. Arjun turned just in time to see Sukhram's body twisting awkwardly before collapsing onto the rocky slope. The impact was immediate, his legs buckling beneath him as he crumpled to the ground. Dust and small stones flew up from the jagged terrain as his body hit the earth with a heavy thud. For a split second, everything seemed to crystallise—Sukhram, once upright and moving with the group, now lay motionless, his face contorted in pain, his rifle slipping from his grasp. The sound of distant gunfire blurred into the background as the reality of the moment settled in. He was down, and there was no time to process it. The mission had to continue, but the sight of Sukhram's fall would remain, a harsh reminder of the ever-present danger they faced.

"Sukhram!" Arjun's voice broke as he scrambled to his side. Blood seeped through Sukhram's uniform, staining the snow beneath him. His eyes fluttered open, and he looked at Arjun with a faint smile.

"Aap aage badho,"[1] Sukhram whispered, his voice barely audible. "Abh yahan ruk ke rone ka time nahi hain humarein paas."[2]

Tears blurred Arjun's vision as he gripped Sukhram's hand, refusing to let go. "I'll get help," he said, his voice shaking.

"No, Sir!," Sukhram said firmly, his grip tightening. "Humein jeetna hain."[3]

Arjun stayed with Sukhram until his grip loosened, his eyes closing for the last time. The loss hit Arjun like a physical blow, but he didn't have the luxury of time to grieve. The mission had to continue. Wiping his tears, Arjun re-joined his unit. Every step upward felt heavier, the weight of one more death pressing down on him. But his grief fuelled his resolve. This wasn't just about the mission anymore; it was about honouring all the sacrifices.

The final assault was a blur of chaos and determination. The unit advanced in small groups, using the terrain for cover as they closed in on the enemy positions. Arjun's world narrowed to the task at hand—clearing one bunker, then another, until the summit was within reach.

As dawn broke over the jagged peaks, casting a pale light on the battlefield, the Indian soldiers launched their final push. The crisp morning air was filled with the deafening sound of gunfire, the clatter of boots, and the heavy thud of artillery. The enemy, entrenched in their positions, fought back with a desperation born of knowing their defeat was imminent. Bullets zipped through the air, striking rocks and earth with deadly precision, but the tide had turned. Arjun, at the forefront, led his group with an intensity that seemed to ignite the very air around him. His movements were swift, almost instinctual, as he dashed from cover to cover, his rifle steady in his hands. Each step forward felt like a tribute to those who had fallen—names and faces flashing through his mind with every pull of the trigger. The enemy's resistance began to falter as the soldiers pressed on relentlessly, closing the gap between themselves and the last of the fortifications. Explosions shook the ground beneath them, sending plumes of smoke into the air, blurring the line between the living and the fallen. Arjun's breath came in ragged gasps, his body battered and aching, but there was no turning back now.

When they reached the summit, the silence was deafening. The Pakistani forces had been overrun, their bunkers cleared. Arjun stood at the peak, his chest heaving, and looked out over the battlefield.

Victory.

Point 5140 was theirs, but the cost was etched in every face, every wound, and every absence. The Indian Army didn't merely stand victorious—they moved quickly to secure their position. They established a defensive perimeter, setting up makeshift shelters amid the rocky outcrops, their rifles still at the ready, scanning the vista for any sign of counterattack. The Bofors artillery, which had been used to pound enemy positions into submission, was now repositioned to provide cover for the advancing soldiers, ensuring that no remnants of resistance would regroup. Signals were sent out immediately to higher command, reporting the success of the operation. The soldiers, though exhausted, continued their vigilance, knowing that holding this strategic peak was just as important as capturing it.

Back in the rest of the country, the news spread swiftly. The media buzzed with reports of the bravery and tenacity displayed by the Indian Army. Point 5140, once a critical stronghold for the enemy, was now in Indian hands. The victory was significant, a turning point in the Kargil conflict. Meera sat in front of the TV, watching intently. The news anchor spoke of victory, the cheers of the crowd echoing in the background. Relief washed over her, yet a deep restlessness remained. Was he safe? Had he survived the battle? Her heart wavered between hope and fear, but she held onto his words—the promise he had made before leaving. He would return to her when the war was over. She clutched the edge of her saree, whispering a silent prayer.

As Arjun stood on the peak, Sameer, like always, beside him, the wind carrying the echoes of battle away, he felt a profound mix of pride and sorrow. The mission was accomplished, but the memories of the climb, the battle, and the comrades who had fallen would stay with him forever. Point 5140 wasn't just a peak; it was a testament to their courage, their unity, and their unwavering commitment to their duty. Kneeling on the cold, jagged ground, he whispered a silent prayer, his lips forming the names of comrades now etched forever in his memory. The unyielding terrain had been a witness to the battle that had raged mere hours ago. The snow was stained with the stories of those who had fought bravely, their sacrifices now part of the very earth beneath his knees. Yet, he saw their smiles of his wife and son in the vastness in front of him, bright and familiar, calling him home. Their laughter echoed in the wind, wrapping around him like a warm embrace.

Yes, the mountain had been reclaimed—its strategic importance secured, its heights once again under the tricolour. Yet, the victory came at a cost that no cheer could erase. The scars it left behind would never fade, carved not just into the land but into their hearts and souls. And yet, as the first rays of the sun broke over Point 5140, bathing the battered soldiers in golden light, Arjun felt an unfamiliar yet quiet sense of peace. They had done their duty. They had honoured their fallen. And in that fleeting moment, as the wind carried their prayers to the heavens, he realised—this mountain would always belong to their memories, but they would never truly leave it behind.

But, there was more.

To the west, Tiger Hill loomed ominously, its sheer heights and well-entrenched enemy positions presenting a challenge that dwarfed even the battles they had fought. Reports were coming in of intense shelling, with Indian troops making painstaking progress under relentless fire. The enemy, desperate and cornered, had fortified their positions with heavy artillery, knowing the loss of Tiger Hill would mark the beginning of the end. Arjun's heart ached for his brothers-in-arms engaged in the brutal struggle there, knowing their triumph was as essential as it was uncertain. The battle for the soul of the mountains was not yet won, and the soldiers steeled themselves for the greater trials that lay ahead.

***

[1]"Keep moving forward."

[2]"Abh yahan ruk ke rone ka time nahi hain humarein paas."

[3]"We have to win."

CHAPTER EIGHT

THE PRICE OF VICTORY

The night after the recapture of Point 5140 was cold but strangely serene. The stars above twinkled like distant spectators, oblivious to the chaos that had unfolded below. Arjun and his comrades lay on the unforgiving rocky ground, their bodies battered, their minds racing with the haunting echoes of battle.

Sameer, lying beside Arjun with his arms tucked behind his head, let out a long, exaggerated sigh. "You know, Arjun," he began, his voice heavy with both exhaustion and a hint of mischief, "if I survive this war, I'm opening a chai stall in Leh. Dras is too tough to reach. Leh will have fresh mountain air, no bullets flying past your ears, just me and my kettle. What do you think?"

Arjun chuckled dryly, shaking his head. "Leh, huh? You'd probably overcharge the tourists and call it 'warrior's chai'."

"Of course!" Sameer grinned, turning his head to look at him. "We've earned the right to overcharge. Every cup would come with a story about how I saved your life on this godforsaken mountain. Twice."

Arjun smirked, rolling his eyes. "Once. And I didn't ask for your help. You just like being a hero."

"Details," Sameer said with a wave of his hand. "The history books won't care. They'll just say Sameer the Brave dragged Arjun the Stubborn out of trouble, under enemy fire, while reciting poetry."

Arjun snorted, wincing slightly as his bruised ribs protested. "Poetry, huh? What's next? You're going to serenade the enemy with your singing?"

"Don't tempt me," Sameer replied, his grin fading slightly as he stared up at the sky. After a pause, he added softly, "You know, I keep hearing Raghav's laugh. Can't get it out of my head."

Arjun sighed, the humour draining from his face. "Me too." He stared at the stars, his voice quieter now. "It's like he's still here. Like he's going to sit up any moment and call us idiots for lying on rocks instead of getting some real sleep."

Sameer smiled faintly, the corners of his mouth twitching. "Yeah, he'd probably say something like, 'If you two have enough energy to joke, you have enough energy to dig a proper trench'."

They both fell silent for a moment, the weight of Raghav's absence settling between them. Finally, Arjun broke the quiet. "You're serious about that tea stall, aren't you?"

"Dead serious," Sameer said with a sigh, his voice tinged with weariness but steady. "And you're going to be my first customer. No discounts, though."

Arjun managed a small laugh, the sound almost foreign in the stillness of the night. "Fine. But if the chai's bad, I'm writing a very detailed complaint. 'Sameer the Brave can't brew a decent cup of tea'."

Sameer chuckled softly, the sound carrying a hint of relief. "Deal. Now shut up and try to sleep, Arjun. Tomorrow's another day, and I'd rather not save your stubborn ass again."

Arjun smiled faintly, closing his eyes, the laughter of a lost friend echoing in his mind as the stars kept silent watch above.

Sleep, that night, though, came in snatches, interrupted by the distant echo of gunfire and the memories of those who had fallen. Faces of their brothers-in-arms haunted Arjun's thoughts—those who had laughed and shared stories in quieter days, were now reduced to memories etched in the unforgiving terrain. The mountain had claimed too many lives, its jagged terrain bearing silent witness to their sacrifices.

Arjun's fingers brushed the dusty ground as he recalled the weight of carrying their fallen down the treacherous slopes, each step laden with sorrow and pride. It wasn't just the enemy they had fought—it was the mountain itself, the biting cold, the thin air, and their own breaking limits. Yet, amidst the exhaustion, there was a flicker of solace. The peak they now rested on stood as a testament to their perseverance. Around him, the others stirred in restless sleep, their breaths visible in the icy air. The sound of a distant mortar reminded them that their fight was far from over. Arjun's glance shifted to the stars, bright and unyielding against the dark sky, and he whispered a silent prayer for strength. Tonight, victory was fragile but theirs. Still, Tiger Hill loomed ahead, a foreboding challenge that promised to test them anew. For now, though, they clung to the memories of their fallen comrades and the quiet resolve to honour them in the battles yet to come.

The orders came at dusk, carried by an officer whose face was as unyielding as the mountains themselves. His voice was steady, almost detached, as he delivered the message that would define their next mission.

"Tiger Hill," he said simply, the words hanging in the freezing air like a challenge.

Arjun felt a jolt of anticipation and dread ripple through the group. The peak loomed in their minds as much as it did in the landscape—a towering sentinel of stone and shadow, its name already whispered with reverence and fear across the battlegrounds.

"Tomorrow night," the officer continued, his eyes scanning the weary but determined faces. "We join the assault. The objective is clear—we take Tiger Hill."

A murmur of acknowledgement passed through the team. Arjun glanced at one of his comrades, who broke the silence with a low whistle. "Tiger Hill, huh? Guess they saved the best for last," he said with a half-smile that didn't quite reach his eyes.

Arjun forced a chuckle but said nothing, his mind racing with questions and memories. The peak had dominated every briefing, its strategic importance drilled into their heads, but now it felt personal. He thought of the men they had lost at Point 5140, their sacrifices echoing in his heart. Would they meet the same fate? Could they endure another climb, another battle, where the odds seemed insurmountable?

Arjun tightened his fists. He looked to the officer, who had already turned to leave, and then to the jagged silhouette of Tiger Hill in the distance. "We'll make it," he said, more to himself than anyone else, the words a quiet vow.

Victory was distant, but the resolve was immediate. Tiger Hill was not just a strategic point; it was a symbol. To reclaim it was to wrest back the dignity of the tricolour and strike a decisive blow in the war.

As they prepared for the mission, the gravity of what lay ahead sank in. The ascent to Tiger Hill would be treacherous—steeper, colder, and deadlier than anything they had faced before. The enemy was deeply entrenched, holding the advantage of height and fortified positions. But the task was clear, and there was no room for hesitation. Arjun looked at his men, their faces lit by the faint glow of a dwindling fire. They were tired, battered by the relentless campaign, but their eyes reflected an unbroken resolve.

The team set out under the cover of darkness, the biting wind slicing through their gear as they climbed the rugged terrain. They moved in silence, each step calculated, each breath measured. As they approached the forward base near Tiger Hill, they met Major Vedant from the 18 Grenadiers, the unit spearheading the charge. Vedant was a towering figure, both in stature and presence, his broad shoulders seeming to carry the weight of the mission itself. His voice had a calm authority that steadied even the most frayed nerves, a quality forged through years of leading men in the harshest terrains. The soldiers of the 18 Grenadiers were known for their grit, having already played a critical role in securing several key positions in the region. Their reputation preceded them, and now, as they prepared for the assault on Tiger Hill, their resolve seemed unshakable.

Vedant approached Arjun and his team with a firm handshake, his eyes sharp but friendly. "You'll be joining us for the final climb," he said with a grin. "Tiger Hill is no walk in the park. The enemy's dug in, and they know we're coming. But don't worry, we've got the 'best' weather for it—freezing winds and plenty of rocks to keep us company." Arjun and Sameer, together, raised an eyebrow each, and Vedant chuckled. "But seriously, it's not going to be easy. We've trained for this, fought for this, and we're going to finish what we started. We're going to take that hill."

Sameer spoke up with a grin, "If the enemy doesn't get us, the wind will."

Vedant gave a mock glare. "Keep it up, and I'll send you first up the hill, no questions asked."

The team laughed quietly, the tension momentarily breaking. Vedant continued, "Look, the truth is, this is the hardest part. But we're not just soldiers out here. We're a team. And there's no one I'd trust more than you guys to get it done. So, let's do this—for the country, for the fallen, and definitely for the bragging rights when we're back at base." He gave a final nod, looking each soldier in the eye. "So, let's go make this hill regret ever standing in our way."

The team, now more at ease, gave a collective nod, ready for the challenge ahead.

Arjun couldn't help but feel a spark of reassurance in Vedant's presence. Around them, the Grenadiers were a flurry of activity—checking weapons, preparing gear, and sharing quiet moments of resolve. Their movements were precise, almost mechanical, a testament to their experience. The gravity of the mission loomed large, but the 18 Grenadiers carried an air of quiet confidence that was infectious. Arjun felt a renewed determination as he looked at Tiger Hill.

"We'll move in coordinated units," Vedant briefed them. "The enemy is dug in deep, with machine guns and mortars ready to cut us down," the officer said, his voice heavy with the weight of experience. "They've rigged false trails with explosives to catch us off guard, and they won't hesitate to draw us into ambushes. Some of our men have been captured mid-ascent. Mortar fire has pinned entire squads, and snipers have picked them off one by one as they tried to retreat. Their bunkers are carved into the rock, nearly impenetrable even under artillery. Make no mistake—this climb isn't just a battle against the mountain; it's a fight against an enemy that knows every cruel trick in the book. But we have the element of surprise. Arjun, your team will flank from the east. It's the most exposed route, but it's also our best chance to break through."

Arjun nodded, his jaw tightening. The east flank meant navigating a near-vertical climb, a sheer wall of rock and ice that seemed to stretch endlessly into the sky. The terrain was unforgiving, its jagged edges sharp enough to cut through boots and gloves, while loose gravel threatened to send even the steadiest climber tumbling into the abyss below. The path offered no cover, just a cruel exposure to the elements and the enemy's watchful eyes. Every step forward would be a gamble, a test of both skill and nerve, with the constant threat of sniper fire or a sudden mortar blast looming over them.

They all knew what lay ahead. They had heard stories of others who had attempted similar climbs—some had made it, their courage immortalised in whispered tales; others had fallen, their cries swallowed by the unforgiving void. It was a path that promised no guarantees, only the hope that their sacrifice would pave the way for victory.

Arjun tightened his grip on his gear, the coarse rope cutting into his palms. His thoughts flickered to those who had already fallen on these mountains, their sacrifices etched into the very rocks they were now tasked to conquer. He looked at his comrades, their faces set with grim determination, and found a flicker of strength in their shared resolve. The climb ahead was daunting, but the stakes were far greater. Tiger Hill awaited, and with it, the chance to honour those who had come before them.

The assault began in the early hours, with the first light of dawn barely piercing the heavy clouds, casting a faint glow on the battlefield. Mortar fire rained down relentlessly as the teams advanced, the earth trembling violently with each explosion, shaking their very core. The air was thick with the acrid smell of gunpowder, mingling with the metallic tang of blood that hung like a ghost over the terrain. Arjun's team pressed forward, every muscle in their bodies burning with the strain, but their resolve only hardened with each step. The icy terrain offered no mercy, its frozen surface a treacherous enemy in itself, making every movement a calculated risk. The enemy's barrage was unyielding, threatening to push them back with every round, but the soldiers held their ground, moving as one. Their training, honed through years of relentless preparation, kicked in, and their rapport, built on unspoken trust and shared purpose, guided them through the chaos. Each step forward was a victory, a testament to their unwavering spirit in the face of overwhelming odds. The cold, the fire, the fear—all became secondary as they moved closer to their objective, a brotherhood bound by a singular mission.

Halfway up the climb, disaster struck with brutal swiftness. A mortar shell exploded nearby, its deafening roar echoing across the desolate landscape. The blast sent shrapnel and jagged debris flying through the air like a storm of death. The ground shook beneath their feet as Arjun's team scrambled to take cover, the icy wind carrying the acrid stench of burning metal and flesh. Through the mist of smoke and dust, Arjun turned in a panic, his heart sinking as he saw one of his men crumple to the ground, his body lifeless before it even hit the snow. Blood stained the white expanse around him, a stark reminder of the unforgiving nature of war. The shock of the loss cut through Arjun like a blade, his mind briefly paralysed by the weight of the moment. But there was no time to mourn, no luxury for grief. The mission pressed on, relentless and unforgiving. Arjun's eyes hardened as his mind snapped back to the present, and he issued orders, his voice steady despite the knot in his throat. The team rallied, pushing through the terror and sorrow, the memory of their fallen comrade fuelling their determination. Each step became heavier, yet they moved forward, bound by duty, knowing the cost of failure was far greater.

As they neared the summit, the fighting intensified. The enemy's fire became more desperate, their attempts to repel the assault growing fiercer. Arjun's team fought with everything they had, their movements a blur of precision and determination. Amid the chaos, he found himself alongside Vedant, who had joined their unit to bolster the attack.

"Arjun," Vedant called out, his voice barely audible over the cacophony of gunfire. "We're close. Push forward. We'll cover you."

Arjun nodded, signalling his team to advance nearer to the cave, his heart pounding in his chest as they charged toward the final stretch. The ground beneath them was slick with blood and mud, the remnants of the fallen telling tales of brutal struggle. As they neared the enemy's caves, the fighting escalated into a savage melee. Hand-to-hand combat erupted, soldiers locking in desperate grapples, their bodies colliding in a blur of violence. The air was thick with the sounds of death—shouts of rage and agony, the sharp crack of gunfire, and the metallic clash of weapons creating an all-consuming cacophony that rattled the senses. Arjun's every move felt instinctive, his training taking over as he parried an incoming strike, his fist connecting with an enemy soldier's jaw with bone-crushing force. The taste of sweat and blood mixed in his mouth as he pushed forward, the roar of combat drowning everything else. In the frenzy, time seemed to stretch, and Arjun felt the air around him thrum with danger, the hairs on his neck standing on end as close calls came at him from all directions. Yet, despite the chaos, his mind remained focused, every breath steady, every motion calculated. The bunker was within reach, but so was the cost of their victory—each passing second felt like it could be their last.

Then, it hit him. A searing pain tore through him. The force knocked him off his feet, sending him tumbling onto the jagged, unforgiving ground. The world around him blurred, the sound of the battle fading into a distant echo.

The damp air in the cave clung to Arjun's skin, cold and heavy like a wet shroud. He tried to move, to shift even slightly, but his body refused to obey. The pain that had once been sharp and searing became distant, dulled to a faint throb, almost as if his senses were slipping away. Time felt warped; seconds stretched into minutes, and minutes into eternity.

Somewhere in the recesses of his mind, he registered the faint sound of water dripping onto the rocky floor, its rhythm steady and unchanging. The sound should have been grounding, but instead, it felt distant, like it belonged to another place entirely. His chest heaved with shallow breaths, each one feeling like a mountain he had to climb.

His thoughts began to drift, unmoored and scattered, like leaves caught in a storm. He felt a strange warmth now, a comforting sensation that didn't match the freezing cold of the cave. It was as though something—someone—was wrapping him in a blanket of calm, pulling him gently away from the biting reality he was in.

A fleeting thought crossed his mind, like a shadow passing over a lake: "*This doesn't feel real*". But the thought was gone as quickly as it came, lost in the fog that had settled over his mind.

Panic clawed at the edges of his mind. Was this it? Was this how it ended?

Then, for just a moment, Arjun thought he heard a voice—soft, familiar, and distant—calling his name. It echoed faintly in the silence of the cave, leaving him unsure if it was real or if his mind was playing tricks on him. His heart stirred weakly, a faint flicker of hope or perhaps a desperate longing for connection.

Faces swam before him, indistinct and shadowed. Were they his comrades or the enemy? For a terrifying moment, he thought he was being dragged away to become a prisoner of war. The thought sent a fresh wave of adrenaline surging through his veins, but it was short-lived. His vision dimmed, and he could no longer tell who held him.

When he opened his eyes again, he saw a group of boys carrying him on what looked like a makeshift stretcher fashioned from wooden planks and tattered cloth. Their faces were smeared with dirt and exhaustion, their eyes burning with determination. He tried to speak, his voice a hoarse whisper. "Where are you taking me?" But his question went unanswered. He felt the stretcher jerk and sway as they manoeuvred through the treacherous terrain.

Summoning what little strength he had, Arjun reached out to one of the boys, his hand trembling. "Listen," he murmured, barely audible over the distant sounds of battle. "Tell my wife about the letters..."

The person nodded solemnly, his expression unreadable, but there was something about him—something familiar. For a fleeting moment, Arjun's heart skipped a beat as he looked into the man's eyes. For some reason, he looked like Raghav—the same sharp features, the same intense look. But Raghav was no more. Arjun's mind screamed at him, trying to shake off the eerie resemblance. He had seen his friend fall, his body lifeless on the ice-covered ground, the blood still fresh. Yet, here was this man, standing in front of him, and for a moment, Arjun couldn't tell if it was grief clouding his judgment or if his mind was playing cruel tricks. He blinked, trying to dispel the image, but the doubt lingered, gnawing at his thoughts.

"I promise," the person said, his voice steady. Arjun's fingers slipped away, and he shut his eyes, the effort of speaking leaving him drained.

His mind drifted in and out of consciousness. Memories flashed before him—his wife's smile, the way the sunlight danced in her hair, the laughter of his young son as he played in the garden. He clung to these images, using them as a lifeline against the encroaching darkness. But the pain was unrelenting, a constant reminder of his fragile grip on life.

The stretcher jolted as the boys carried him over uneven ground, and he winced, the movement sending fresh waves of agony through his body. He could hear snippets of their hurried conversation.

"We have to get him to the medic..."

"The enemy's still firing, we'll be sitting ducks if we stay here too long."

"Keep moving! He's losing too much blood."

Arjun tried to focus on their words, but his thoughts kept drifting. He thought of the men who had fallen beside him, their faces a blur now, but their courage still vivid. He thought of the officer's briefing, the dire warnings that had come true in the most brutal ways. And he thought of the mountain itself, its unforgiving slopes a silent witness to their struggle.

He opened his eyes again, just briefly, and saw the faint outline of a tent in the distance, barely visible against the unforgiving landscape. His mind swirled with confusion and disbelief. How had they reached such a low altitude? The climb had been treacherous, and yet, here he was, staring at this uncertain sight. Had he been carried all this way? His body felt strangely weightless in his thoughts. His foggy mind couldn't piece together the fragments of the journey. Why had the others been left behind in the ice, their fates sealed by the relentless cold? He couldn't understand. Was this a medic's post or was it just another cruel illusion, born from the fading threads of his consciousness? The line between reality and hallucination blurred, and fear crept into his heart. All he could do was grasp desperately at the fragments of clarity. His vision grew dim again, but in that fleeting moment, he trusted in the boys who had carried him. Their resolve, their unwavering spirit, was as firm as the mountains they had scaled, and he clung to that certainty as he drifted back into the haze.

"Hold on!" one of them said, his voice breaking through the blur. "We're almost there."

Arjun wanted to respond, to tell them he was grateful, but the words wouldn't come. Instead, he let himself drift. The battle for Tiger Hill raged on in the distance, a brutal reminder that their mission was far from over. But for now, all he could do was hold onto the promise of another sunrise, another chance to fight, another chance to return home.

***

CHAPTER NINE

TIME TO RETURN HOME

He opened his eyes slowly, the effort feeling like dragging himself through thick mud. His eyelids were heavy as if they had been glued shut, and his vision blurred as he tried to focus. The light around him flickered, opening and shutting, as if the world itself couldn't decide whether it was day or night. He blinked again, trying to clear the haze in his mind, but it only seemed to deepen the confusion.

The first thing he noticed was the chill. A coldness seeped into his bones, leaving him shivering. The cold wrapped around him like a blanket of ice, and he instinctively curled into himself, seeking warmth. But no matter how much he tried to move, his limbs felt heavy, unresponsive, as though they no longer belonged to him. His chest tightened with a dull ache, and the air seemed to press down on him, thick and suffocating.

He glanced around, trying to make sense of his surroundings. The walls around him were blurry, shifting in and out of focus. It looked like a tent, but not one he recognised. The fabric was torn in places, a patchwork of material that didn't seem to belong together. His mind screamed for answers, but all he could grasp were fragments. A tent. A battlefield. Ice. His body, frozen in place. But the more he thought, the less clear everything became.

The cold. It was the cold that overwhelmed him first. He could feel it seeping through his clothes, biting at his skin, as though he were lying on solid ice. His fingers twitched as he tried to move, his mind commanding his body to respond, but it took a moment before his hands even twitched in acknowledgement. He wanted to sit up, to look around, to understand where he was, but his body betrayed him. He felt too weak, too exhausted.

Slowly, painfully, he forced himself to turn his head, scanning his surroundings. The tent's interior was dim, lit only by the faint glow of a lantern hanging from the centre pole. There was a heavy silence, the kind that presses down on you, making the air feel thick and suffocating. He could hear nothing but the sound of his own breathing, shallow and ragged, as though his lungs were struggling to take in the air. There was no sound of battle, no distant gunfire or explosions. Just silence. The kind of silence that followed chaos, the kind that settled in after the storm had passed.

He tried to sit up again, the effort causing his body to tremble with weakness. His chest burned with every movement, each breath coming in short, painful gasps. He felt something sharp digging into his side, and when he reached down to touch it, his fingers brushed against the cold steel of a medical bandage wrapped tightly around his torso. The realisation hit him like a punch in the gut. He was injured. Badly. There had been a wound. A deep, searing pain. But now, as he touched the bandages, he only felt the dull ache of healing.

The memory came rushing back in fragments. The battlefield. The mortar fire. The chaos. He had been in the thick of it. Fighting. Surviving. But then... then there had been an explosion. A flash of light. The shockwave. He remembered feeling the ground tremble beneath him, the air thick with smoke and dust, and the sharp, metallic taste of blood in his mouth. And then... nothing. His mind had gone blank.

He closed his eyes, trying to push away the panic that began to rise within him. He had to focus. He had to remember. He couldn't let his mind spiral into a mess of confusion and fear. Slowly, he took a deep breath, his chest screaming in protest, and tried to steady himself. The cold was unbearable, but it was also grounding.

It reminded him that he was still alive. That he had made it through whatever hell he had just been through. He wasn't dead. He was still here.

But where was here?

His mind raced, trying to make sense of the disjointed memories. The last thing he remembered clearly was the battle—the mortar fire, the explosions, the screams. The ice-cold winds of the mountains. But then... there had been darkness. The kind of darkness that swallowed everything, leaving nothing but an empty void. How had he ended up here? Had he been rescued? Or was he still trapped in some kind of twisted, nightmarish reality? Was he even awake?

He tried to call out, but his voice came out as a rasp, barely more than a whisper. "Hello?" he croaked. His voice sounded foreign to him, weak and hoarse, as though he hadn't spoken in days. He waited for a response, straining his ears to hear anything that would tell him he wasn't alone. But there was nothing. Only the eerie silence, as if the world itself was holding its breath.

His body was still immobile, as though it refused to cooperate. The cold had numbed him, and the pain in his chest was a constant reminder of how close he had come to death. But somehow, his mind refused to give in. It clung to the fragments of his memories, trying to piece together what had happened. The battle. His men. The fight. The victory. But the more he tried to recall, the more fragmented everything became.

He closed his eyes again, trying to push away the confusion. He had to focus. He had to understand where he was. What had happened? He had to know if his team had made it out alive. Had they won? Or had they lost? Were they still fighting? Were they still out there?

The cold pressed against his skin, but it wasn't as suffocating as the fear that began to churn in his gut. What had happened to them? To his comrades? What had happened to the battle?

In the dim light of the tent, he heard the faintest rustle of movement. It was barely audible, but it was enough to snap him out of his thoughts. His head whipped around, his eyes darting to the source of the sound. But there was nothing. Only the shadows stretching across the tent, the ghostly shapes of medical supplies and equipment. No one was there. Not even a single person to answer his questions, to tell him what was happening.

The silence returned, even heavier this time. And the cold seemed to invade every part of him, from his bones to his very soul. It was the kind of cold that made you question if you were even alive, or if you had crossed over into some cold, indifferent afterlife. He swallowed hard, trying to force the panic back down. He had to focus. He had to keep it together.

He tried to move again, this time more carefully, testing his body's limits. His arms were weak, his legs trembling, but he was determined to sit up. Slowly, agonisingly, he pulled himself into a sitting position. His head swam with dizziness, and his vision blurred, but he forced himself to stay conscious. The cold was unbearable, but it was also a reminder that he was still here. He was still alive.

There was a rustle again, louder this time. Footsteps. Someone was coming. He turned his head toward the sound, his heart pounding in his chest. His eyes strained, and he saw a figure emerge from the shadows—a silhouette against the dim light. It was hard to make out at first, but as the figure drew closer, the details became clearer.

It was a medic. A man in a military uniform, his face obscured by a mask, but his presence was reassuring. The medic knelt beside him, placing a hand gently on his shoulder.

"Arjun?" A soft voice broke through the obscurity. A figure appeared at the side of his bed—a doctor, perhaps. He couldn't focus long enough to see clearly. The figure reached out and pressed a cool hand to his forehead, then began speaking in a calm, steady tone. "Take it easy. You've been through a lot."

He blinked, trying to speak, but the words felt like they were trapped somewhere deep inside him, unable to escape. His throat was dry and raw, and his mouth felt thick, as though he hadn't spoken in days. But even through the fogginess, his mind raced. Where was he? What had happened? His hand twitched. He wanted to speak, but the words wouldn't come. He managed to croak something, barely audible. "Where... where am I?"

The person's face appeared above him, a faint shadow of concern crossing his features. "You're safe Arjun. You've been unconscious for several days... I know you want to go home... You will..."

Days? The word didn't register immediately. He had no memory of how long he'd been here, how he'd ended up in this sterile, lifeless place. His mind was too foggy to make sense of the passage of time. He tried to remember the last moments before he had lost consciousness. His body ached as he recalled the cold, the violence, the battle. The battle... The thought flashed in his mind like a bolt of lightning. He had been in the thick of it, hadn't he? He had been fighting, fighting for everything. The memory of the carnage, the chaos, gripped him tightly. The air had been thick with smoke, the ground littered with debris, and the sound of gunfire and explosions had been deafening. Yet now... now there was nothing but silence.

"The battle..." he muttered, his voice barely a whisper. "What happened? How...?"

The person gently placed a hand on his shoulder, a subtle but firm gesture to stop him from trying to sit up. "You've been through a lot, Arjun. It has been a week... One at a time... Get ready for home..."

A week? His mind reeled. A week? But he hadn't been aware of even a single moment passing. He had no memory of being carried off the battlefield, no recollection of being brought here. He tried to focus, but the pain in his chest was overwhelming. He could feel the tightness, the pressure—a constant reminder of how close he had come to death. But why had he survived? Why had he been spared? He couldn't wrap his head around it.

And what was it about this voice? Soft yet commanding, it carried an otherworldly calmness, stirring something deep within Arjun. More than sound, it was a pull—gentle, undeniable. He couldn't even see the face. Was this the doctor? Or someone else? He wasn't even sure where he was anymore.

"I need to go back..." His voice was hoarse, but the urgency in his tone was unmistakable. He tried to push himself up, but the pain in his chest intensified, and he collapsed back onto the bed, gasping for air.

The person shook his head gently, his expression soft yet firm. "You need to rest. The battle is over, Arjun. India has won."

India has won. The words didn't make sense. His mind was a storm of thoughts and confusion. How could it be over? How could the battle be over? He had been there, in the trenches, every moment soaked in the weight of war. He had fought with everything he had, watching comrades fall, feeling the sting of loss with every step forward. The faces of those who had bled beside him haunted him, their cries reverberating in the silent corners of his mind. He thought of the chaos—the explosions, the gunfire, the blood—and now, an eerie calm had settled in. "Victory is not always loud," he thought, but even the silence seemed foreign, unsettling. Everything he knew had been defined by the battle, and now the world was telling him it was over. He had braved the worst, had seen the darkness of war up close, yet now, he was here—lying in a bed, while outside the world had changed. "I was a part of it," he thought, "I was there." But this quiet felt wrong. Had he missed something? Was this peace, or was he still trapped in the chaos of his own mind? How could something so monumental end so quietly, with no fanfare, no closure?

"I was there," Arjun muttered very slowly and very softly; his voice breaking. "I was fighting... How is it over?"

The man's expression softened as he sat beside the bed, his hand resting gently on Arjun's head. The touch was soft, comforting, as if he understood Arjun's pain without a word. It carried warmth, a quiet reassurance that he wasn't alone. In that moment, Arjun felt a flicker of peace amidst the confusion. "The battle ended days ago, Arjun. The war is over. It's time for you to heal."

How could it be over? How could he have missed it all? He had been in the midst of a fight, a struggle for survival, and now he was being told that it was over? The weight of it pressed down on him, and a deep, gnawing sense of loss began to settle in his chest. His comrades, his brothers in arms—had they made it? Had they survived? What had happened to them? The guilt gnawed at him, sharper than any physical pain he had ever felt. Why had he survived when so many hadn't? Why had he made it when so many others had fallen? The thought was suffocating. He couldn't breathe. His chest tightened, and his heart seemed to stop beating for a moment.

"I need to know," he said, his voice shaky. "What happened to my men?"

The person hesitated, then spoke softly. "Your team fought bravely. Many of them made it out alive, but not all. You lost some of your brothers out there. It was a brutal battle. But India won, Arjun. We won."

India won... The words echoed in his mind, but they didn't bring the relief he had expected. Instead, they deepened the emptiness inside him. What was a victory if it came at such a cost? What was the point of winning if so many had died? The faces of his fallen comrades—his team, his brothers—flashed in his mind like haunting spectres. They were gone. And yet, here he was, alive, breathing, but carrying the weight of their sacrifice. It was like the aftermath of every war, from the trenches of World War I to the battlefields of modern-day conflicts—a victory forever tainted by loss. What had they truly gained if the soil was soaked with the blood of the fallen? Victory felt like a hollow shell, a trophy won by the living but never fully grasped. As the flowers of peace bloomed in the distance, all Arjun could see were the letters written by families, their words of hope and pride now forever unanswered. The smell of gunpowder still clung to the air, and the memories of those who died remained etched in his soul. War, he realised, took more than lives—it took pieces of the soul, the fragments of joy, the warmth of human connection. What was the point of a world that moved on when so many were left behind?

In the days to come, many stories would emerge from the ashes of the Kargil War. Tales of men who had given everything for the nation—some celebrated, others quietly forgotten until unearthed by grieving families. The stories of Kargil's heroes extend far beyond the names etched into history books. While iconic moments like a major's fearless battle cry, "Yeh dil maange more"[1] have become the essence of valour, it is the lesser-told narratives that reveal the true depth of sacrifice. Soldiers charged at enemy positions despite life-threatening wounds, scaling sheer cliffs under relentless fire, embodying raw courage and unwavering dedication. Some endured unimaginable suffering, becoming symbols of resilience in the face of brutality. For every celebrated act of heroism, countless other sacrifices remained known only to grieving families. A soldier's wife waited for years, hoping against hope, until skeletal remains confirmed his fate. Her solace lay in finally being able to offer him a proper resting place. A father, each year, climbed the same unforgiving peaks where his son had fought and fallen, seeking solace in retracing his final steps. For others, closure was denied entirely. Families received bloodied belongings but no body, while Pakistan refused to claim their own fallen soldiers. The Indian Army, in a profound act of humanity, buried the enemy dead with dignity, even as their own grief ran deep.

War does not end when the last shot is fired. It leaves behind scars—some visible, others buried deep within hearts and memories. For the men on the frontlines, it takes away the simplicity of life, replacing it with a haunting awareness of its fragility. For families, it is a void that no medals or honours can fill. Letters that once carried love and pride sit like relics of a life interrupted. Flowers placed on graves cannot speak to the dreams cut short. The Kargil War, while a moment of pride for India, was also a chapter written in tears and blood.

Arjun thought, "Victory has come, yes, but at a cost so profound that it could never be fully reckoned. It has brought India together, igniting patriotism and a sense of shared purpose. Yet, it also remains the nation of the grim realities of war. Lives have been lost, families shattered, and a generation of soldiers carried wounds—physical and emotional—that time will never truly heal."

Truly, to this day, the Kargil victory stands as a testament to India's resilience and valour, but it also serves as a sombre reminder of what war takes away. It is a victory that will forever shine in history, but its glow is tinged with the shadows of sacrifice.

Arjun closed his eyes, his mind a battlefield of its own. He didn't know how long he lay there, but eventually, a sense of acceptance began to seep into him. The battle was over. It was time to go home.

***

[1]"This heart wants more."

CHAPTER TEN

BETWEEN TWO WORLDS

The chugging of the train became a soothing lullaby as Arjun leaned back against the window, his uniform a silent reminder of the battle he had left behind. The war—its chaos, its screams, its heart-stopping moments—was now a memory that felt both vivid and distant. He had spent months in the frosty heights, where every breath was a struggle, and every moment a battle for survival. Yet, even in the harshest of conditions, life found moments of humour. Like the time one of the younger soldiers tried to make tea in the biting cold, only to have the water ice-over halfway to boiling, leaving the entire team laughing as they teased him about his 'frozen chai'. Or the day a mischief-maker carved a snowman wearing a sergeant's hat, complete with a makeshift rifle, earning both laughter and a playful reprimand. But the war was never far from their thoughts. There was the night when mortar fire rained down unexpectedly, and Arjun had to drag a wounded comrade to safety, their hands slipping on the blood-soaked snow as the man gasped for air. Then, there was the brutal memory of storming an enemy position, the chaos of hand-to-hand combat searing itself into his mind—the metallic tang of blood, the cries of the fallen, and the devastating realisation that some of his men would never return. These moments—both light-hearted and harrowing—etched themselves into his soul, a reminder of the fragile line between life and death in the mountains.

But now was here; seated in a train compartment filled with the hum of normalcy, as if the war had been a distant dream. It was almost surreal.

Arjun's thoughts drifted to his childhood, the simpler days of running through mustard fields, climbing mango trees, and sneaking sweets from the kitchen when his mother wasn't looking. Those were days of unbridled freedom, of innocence untouched by the weight of duty or the shadow of loss. He thought of his father's stern yet loving gaze, the way he had taught him to fly kites with precision, and his mother's gentle hands combing his hair, chiding him for coming home muddy yet always ready with a plate of steaming parathas. These memories felt like an anchor, pulling him back to a time when life was uncomplicated and his biggest worry was a scraped knee.

But now, life had transformed him into a soldier, a protector of the nation, carrying scars both visible and invisible. The war had tested his resolve in ways he had never imagined, and yet it was the thought of his family that had kept him going. His wife's face came to his mind—her warm smile, the way her eyes lit up when she teased him about his terrible singing and the memory of her holding their son for the first time. Their child was just one year old now, barely old enough to remember his father. Arjun's heart ached for him. The thought tugged at his heart, filling him with a strange mixture of longing and anxiety. His hand instinctively went to his chest, where the dull ache of his healing wound lingered—a constant reminder of both his survival and his fragility. Would he be able to hold his tiny baby in his arms without wincing in pain? Would he have the strength to lift him high, to hear his giggles and feel the warmth of his small hands on his face? His mind strayed to his wife, her smile a distant memory he had clung to in the cold. Would he be able to touch her, to love her the way he used to, or had war left him too broken? His fingers brushed against his face, now rough with the beard he had grown in the mountains. He hadn't shaved since the day they'd been called to the front. Would his son find it funny, or would he cry, confused by the man who looked so different from the photographs? These questions, mundane yet deeply personal, swirled in his mind, carrying with them the weight of hope and an undercurrent of fear.

The train compartment was a microcosm of life in peacetime India—vibrant, noisy, and blissfully unaware. A young couple nearby shared a tiffin, the aroma of spicy aloo parathas wafting through the air. They laughed over some inside joke, their heads close together as if the world outside didn't exist. Arjun's mind wandered to the makeshift meals at the base camp. The food there had been a functional necessity, not a moment of joy. He thought of Nikhil, who once cracked a joke about their perpetually cold rotis, saying, "If the enemy doesn't kill us, the food will." That memory brought a flicker of a smile to his face, but it quickly faded. Nikhil would never complain about another meal again.

In another corner, a group of children clapped in rhythm, their voices growing louder with each round of their game. Their innocent joy filled the compartment like music, but for Arjun, it was a jarring reminder of the silence that had defined his days in Kargil. The sound of clapping hands was eerily similar to the burst of gunfire. He instinctively tensed, his mind flashing back to the climb to Point 5140, where every sound was scrutinised, every movement deliberate. One had clapped his hands together to warm them during a bitterly cold night, only to be met with stern glares. "You want to announce our position to the enemy?" Another had hissed. Now, the children's game seemed both haunting and absurdly carefree.

An elderly man on the upper bunk adjusted his glasses, engrossed in his newspaper. Headlines about Kargil were splashed across the front page, but the man barely seemed to register them. Arjun wondered if the words conveyed the reality of what had happened—the freezing nights, the relentless shelling, the friends who had fallen. He remembered a soldier who had joked, "At least we won't have to read about this in the papers. We're living it." That dark humour had carried them through some of the worst moments, but now, seeing the man's indifference, it stung in a way he hadn't expected. Did people even understand what those headlines meant?

The train stopped at a small station, and vendors poured in. "Chai, chai garam!" they called, balancing flasks and trays of steaming cups. Arjun didn't buy the tea. He knew exactly how it would taste—weak, overly sweet, and a far cry from what he had grown accustomed to. On the battlefield, tea was a lifeline, brewed in battered tin mugs over fires that barely took hold in the thin mountain air. It wasn't about flavour; it was about warmth, a fleeting comfort in the relentless cold. The thought of that smoke-tinged bitterness made him almost nostalgic. Here, the vendor's sugary concoction, poured hurriedly into paper cups, seemed more a luxury than a necessity, yet it lacked the grit and purpose of those battlefield brews. He thought of Baldev who had once tried to add condensed milk to their tea ration, only to spill the entire can. "Lagta hai, aaj kaali chai hi naseeb mein likha hain,"[1] he had said, laughing at his own blunder. The memory was both amusing and painful—his mate's voice now a ghost in his mind.

Another vendor passed by with a tray of fried snacks, the scent of samosas mingling with the sweat and leather of the compartment. Arjun's stomach tightened. The smell reminded him of the rations they'd opened after capturing Point 5140—half-frozen packets of dal and rice that tasted like victory, despite their blandness. One had taken one bite and declared, "This is worse than enemy fire." Everyone had laughed then, the tension of battle momentarily broken. Now, surrounded by the rich smells of civilian life, Arjun couldn't help but feel the stark divide between then and now.

The children's laughter rose again, and Arjun glanced at them, their carefree existence almost alien to him. The idea that life could be this simple, this untouched by the weight of sacrifice, was both comforting and haunting. He thought of the soldiers who had fought alongside him, their smiles and jokes masking fear, their lives cut short so that these children could play games in peace.

Arjun observed it all, his eyes taking in the mundane details that he had once taken for granted. He had fought for this—for these ordinary moments, for people to live their lives without fear. Yet, the contrast between the life he had left behind and the life he was returning to felt almost jarring.

As the train rolled into a station, a group of young men entered the compartment, chatting animatedly about cricket and college exams. One of them brushed past Arjun, his shoulder grazing the uniformed arm that rested on the seat's edge, but he didn't even glance at him. Arjun looked up, expecting a fleeting acknowledgement, perhaps even a curious remark about his presence. Instead, the boys settled into their seats and continued their chatter, their laughter rising above the hum of the train. It was as though he were invisible. He shifted slightly, but still, there was no reaction. Were they deliberately avoiding him? Did the uniform intimidate them, or had the horrors of the war, so vividly painted by the media, made soldiers a symbol of something they didn't want to confront?

Later, as the train slowed down to another halt, a middle-aged couple entered with their teenage daughter. The father, holding a newspaper folded neatly under his arm, glanced momentarily in Arjun's direction. Their eyes met for a fraction of a second before the man looked away, ushering his family into their seats. Arjun noticed the newspaper headlines—blurred images of soldiers, victory, and loss—but no words were exchanged. The girl, perched on the edge of her seat, whispered something to her mother, who gave a quick, almost furtive look in his direction and then turned away. For a moment, Arjun wondered if the look had even been meant for him, realising she might not have even been looking at him at all! Perhaps her gaze had fallen on the vendor standing at the station, visible through the window, arranging his wares with practised ease. The thought unsettled him; the uncertainty of being noticed—or ignored—left him adrift in his own presence.

He had expected questions, curious glances—something—maybe even admiration for the uniform he wore. But there was none of that. Were people scared of soldiers now, associating them only with violence and tragedy? Or did they simply want to forget these past months, to leave the war behind as a distant nightmare? The thought gnawed at him, land yet, oddly enough, at some level he was grateful for it. Their indifference gave him a sense of peace. He didn't have to relive the war through their questions or try to put into words the unspeakable things he had seen and done.

He spent most of the journey staring out of the window. The landscape outside was a blur of greens and browns, villages and fields passing by like a moving painting. He saw farmers bent over their crops, children playing by the roadside, and women carrying pots of water on their heads. It was a world so far removed from the icy heights and the deafening roar of mortar shells that it felt almost unreal. He found himself longing for the ordinary—to sit on a charpoy under the shade of a banyan tree, to sip tea from an earthen cup, to hear the distant call of a temple bell.

The bus journey from the medical camp to the train station had drained him. His body ached from the wounds that were still healing, and his mind felt heavy with exhaustion. But this journey, this return to normalcy, was what he had yearned for during the long nights in the trenches. He had imagined this moment countless times—and it had come.

When Arjun opened his eyes, he didn't know when he had fallen asleep. The rhythmic hum of the train, combined with the gentle sway, had lulled him into a peaceful slumber. The sudden halt of the train startled him awake. Blinking, he noticed the train had stopped, and his destination had come. His home was now only a half-hour away, just one last bus ride. He grabbed his bag, feeling the jolt of excitement and weariness at the same time. The doors opened, and he stepped off, heading towards the bus that awaited him at the platform.

The bus ride jostled its passengers like dice in a cup, each pothole a reminder of just how familiar this route was to Arjun. He sat by the window, his stare fixed on the passing fields, the occasional roadside temple, and the clusters of houses that made up his hometown. The rhythmic squeak of the windowpane matched the vehicle's groans over uneven roads, a melody of discomfort that was oddly soothing in its predictability. The conductor moved down the aisle, a weathered figure in a faded uniform, calling out stops with a voice that carried authority and weariness. Arjun's hand instinctively reached for his pocket before he remembered—his wallet was gone, likely left behind during the chaos of his return journey. He braced himself to explain, perhaps even crack a joke about soldiers getting a free pass home, but the conductor's glance lingered just long enough and then, without a word, the man moved on, leaving Arjun both relieved and slightly embarrassed. The simple gesture, unspoken yet deeply felt, brought a small lump to his throat.

The bumpy ride brought back memories of a different kind of journey—one far less forgiving. Arjun thought of the truck rides he had taken during his deployment, the open-top vehicles rumbling precariously along narrow mountain passes. Those rides were bone-rattling in their own right, the uneven terrain making every bump feel like an assault. Unlike the bus, there were no cushioned seats, just wooden planks that dug into the soldiers' backs. The air had been biting, the kind of cold that sliced through layers of gear and left lips cracked and fingers numb. Yet, there had been bonding in that shared discomfort—jokes shouted over the roar of the engine.

On those trucks, the soldiers had shared more than just space. Meals were rationed, but stories were abundant. Someone would always pull out a harmonica or hum a tune, their voices blending with the wind's howl. They'd pass around a shared thermos of chai, its warmth a brief respite from the freezing air. The smell of diesel mixed with the faint tang of sweat and gun oil was a sensory cocktail Arjun could never forget. The sharp turns and steep ascents had been terrifying, but those truck rides had also been moments of incredible unity. There, on the edge of danger, they had found fragments of normalcy—a crude joke, a laugh, or a shared glance that said, "We're in this together."

He got off, his heart thudding with anticipation as he walked the short distance to his home. The familiar route felt comforting, yet different. It wasn't his childhood home, but it had become his sanctuary after marriage. As he walked, he passed the old tea shop where the vendor still served his strong chai, the aroma filling the air, making his stomach rumble. The local bookstore, with its wooden sign swaying in the breeze, was a place he and his wife often visited, browsing through novels on quiet afternoons. The sound of children playing cricket in the park nearby made him smile, remembering how they'd often sit on the same bench, watching the games with a cup of coffee in hand. The familiar buzz of the neighbourhood, with its friendly chatter and the hum of radios from nearby shops, reminded him of the life they had built here together. It felt like the world had been waiting for him to return.

Finally, as he arrived in front of the house, his steps slowed, taking in the sight of the familiar door that had seen better days. A deep scratch marred the wood just below the brass handle, its edges worn smooth over time. Arjun ran his fingers over it, a grin tugging at his lips as he remembered the incident. It wasn't the kids playing cricket or an accidental knock—it was the aftermath of a clumsy moment between him and his wife. One hurried, stolen kiss in the doorway, and her high heels had scraped against the door as they stumbled inside, laughing like teenagers. The memory warmed him, the thought of her playful scolding afterwards as she declared it was his fault for being 'too eager', making him chuckle.

To the left of the door sat a flower pot, the same one where they'd always hidden the spare key, though anyone could have guessed it by now. The pot was slightly off-kilter, its terracotta rim chipped from when it had been knocked over during one of their late-night conversations on the porch. He bent down to straighten it, his hand briefly brushing the cool soil within, and smiled at the marigolds she loved so much. He could not straighten it. He tried again but he was unable to life it. He placed his hand on his chest. He looked at the pot again. He knew.

He rang the doorbell, the chime echoing through the stillness of the evening. Inside, he could hear the shuffle of hurried footsteps, the familiar sound of her shoes on the tiled floor. For a moment, he stood there, hand lingering on the bell, savouring the moment. The door opened, and there she was—her hair slightly mussed and her eyes lighting up at the sight of him. The scratch on the door, the flower pot, even the ache in his chest—all of it faded away as he stepped into her arms, into the warmth of home. She was the one person who could instantly quiet the whirlwind inside him, making everything feel right again.

He was finally home.

***

[1]"Looks like black tea is all that's in my fate today."

THE TRUTH

She stood there, stunned. Arjun was right in front of her, as real as the air she breathed. For weeks, she had tried to find out about him, clinging to every shred of hope. And now, without warning, he was here—standing just a few feet away. Her heart pounded in disbelief, her breath caught in her throat. Then, as if all the longing, fear, and desperation had built up into this one moment, she flung herself at him, wrapping her arms around him as if she would never let go.

"I thought I had lost you," she said, her voice thick with emotion. Her arms clung to him, as if afraid to let go, as though her embrace could somehow anchor him to her, make him real again. Arjun held her just as tightly, his own heart racing as the weight of everything they had both endured crashed down on him. His chest ached, not just from the physical toll of the past months, but from the sheer joy of being home, of being held by her again.

"I'm here," he whispered back, his voice hoarse. "I'm here now."

For a long moment, they just stood there, locked in each other's arms, the world outside fading away. The last few months, the uncertainty, the fear—it all felt like a distant memory as he breathed in her warmth, her scent, the comfort of his home. She pulled back slightly, her hands gently cupping his face, her eyes searching his as if to make sure he was really there, that this wasn't just some dream.

Tears welled up in her eyes, but she smiled through them, a soft, trembling smile of relief. "When I heard you had taken a bullet... I didn't know what to think. I couldn't find out where you were...

people said all sorts of things—some said you were lost, others said you were dead. I didn't know if you were alive or gone... But I prayed, Arjun. I prayed every day that you'd come back."

Her words hit him like a wave. All the fear she had endured, the uncertainty, it was all there in her voice. Arjun felt a lump form in his throat, and he held her tighter, wanting to shield her from all the pain she had carried. "I'm sorry," he murmured. "I never meant to hurt you. But I'm here now."

She nodded, her tears slipping down her cheeks, but her smile remained steady. "I knew you were strong," she whispered. "I knew you'd come back to me."

Arjun kissed her forehead gently, overwhelmed with gratitude that she hadn't given up on him. He felt her forehead on his lips, just as he had felt her embrace. He smiled—when you truly love someone, every touch is felt, no matter what. It's like magic, like energies colliding to make it happen.

When they finally pulled back, she led him into the living room, her hand resting on his arm as though she never wanted to let him out of her sight. The house felt different now—quieter, but filled with the promise of a new beginning.

She settled him onto the couch and went to the kitchen, and within moments, the smell of freshly brewed masala tea filled the air. Arjun sighed in contentment, the scent taking him back to simpler times. His wife returned, a steaming cup in hand, her eyes still full of warmth and relief.

"You always know how to make everything better," he said, his voice soft as he gestured her to keep the cup on the table. He knew he would not be able to hold it.

She smiled, sitting beside him, her hand slipping into his. "It's your favourite," she said, her fingers tracing the lines of his palm. "I made it just the way you like it."

She sipped the tea in comfortable silence for a few moments—Arjun's still untouched—before the conversation began to flow—slowly at first, then with more urgency, as though they were trying to catch up on years of missing time. Arjun shared the harrowing details of his time away and how, through it all, he had kept one thought close: the hope of coming home to her.

She listened intently, her eyes never leaving his face. "When I heard about the victory, I couldn't stop myself. I called everyone I could, hoping someone would tell me you were okay. But no one could give me an answer. Two days passed, and still, you didn't come home." Her eyes welled with tears as she continued, her gaze fixed on him. "Then they said you had died in a cave, that you were trapped, and they couldn't get to you. They told me to wait because sending people to recover bodies in such places wasn't a priority." She paused, her voice breaking. "Do you know what it felt like to be told to wait? To imagine you, all alone in that cave, and know they wouldn't come for you?" Her voice broke slightly, but she quickly composed herself. "The neighbours were kind, Arjun. They looked after me. But it wasn't the same. It wasn't you."

Arjun squeezed her hand, feeling the weight of her loneliness. "I'm sorry," he said again. "I know I wasn't there, but I was always thinking of you... of both of you."

Her face softened as she nodded. "I know. And the boy... he missed you so much. Every day, he'd ask where his daddy was. It broke my heart to see him waiting, hoping for you to come home."

Arjun's chest tightened at the thought of their son.

Meera looked at him silently, taking him in, her eyes tracing the lines on his face that spoke of battles fought and endured. His once vibrant eyes were now shadowed, possibly clouded with memories of pain and loss. The man she had waited for, the one she had dreamed of coming home, seemed both familiar and foreign in the same breath. She couldn't help but notice the faint scar on his cheek, a silent testimony to the harsh realities he had faced. Her heart swelled with emotions she couldn't quite name—relief, sorrow, fear, and something else, something deeper, that she hadn't felt in years.

"They said you were hit by a bullet.... I-I couldn't believe it. They said you had been left behind... in a cave, Arjun. That you had... that you had died."

She was repeating herself, her voice trembling each time. Each word felt like a desperate attempt to anchor herself to the man she thought she had lost forever. Arjun could see the fear in her eyes, the pain of a wound that time hadn't healed, and the unspoken weight of everything she had gone through in his absence. He understood, perhaps more deeply than anyone else could, the torment of not knowing, of waiting in silence for something that might never come. Even as she asked again, his heart ached for her, knowing that no words could fully erase the uncertainty she had lived with.

He sighed deeply, the air around him heavy with memories of that night. "Meera, I am here.... We were holed up inside an enemy cave, trapped with no clear way out, no way to fight back. The bullet.... it hit me. It tore through and I went down hard. For a moment, everything went dark."

"I was told that... that you were too far gone to be saved. That they had to leave you there, Arjun. That you were... left behind." Her voice cracked, and her eyes filled with sorrowful disbelief. "How could they have left you there?"

Arjun looked at her, his heart heavy with the weight of the truth. "She deserved answers, but how can I give them without breaking her completely?"

Her tears stung his very being.

Meera's voice faltered, her eyes searching his face for signs of the pain he had endured. "How did you survive, Arjun? How did they keep you alive? I... I don't understand. The bullet... it sounded like it was... it sounded like it would have been fatal."

He shifted suddenly, his tone lighter, almost forced. "Enough about that. How have you been holding up these past few days? I'm sure you've been running around, trying to take care of everything, haven't you?" The change in subject was abrupt, almost jarring, but he masked it with a faint smile. **She can't know. Not yet.** The thought echoed in his mind, a silent plea.

Meera blinked, caught off guard by his sudden pivot. "Arjun, you're avoiding something. What aren't you telling me?"

But he only shook his head, his expression unreadable. "Some things are better left unsaid, Meera. For now."

"I thought I had lost you, Arjun. I thought the worst had happened. And there was nothing I could do. No way to reach you, no way to help. The waiting, the not knowing... it nearly broke me."

Arjun's heart clenched as he saw the pain in her eyes. He gently placed his hand over hers, holding it against his cheek. "I know, Meera. I know. I'm sorry. I never wanted you to go through that. But you're here now, and I'm here. We're both here. And that's all that matters. We can't change the past, but we can make sure the future is different."

Tears slipped down her cheeks. "I don't care about anything else, Arjun. I don't care about the war, the fights, the pain. I only care about you. You're alive, and that's all that matters."

"I'm home, Meera. I'm finally home."

As the evening wore on, they continued to talk—about everything that had happened, about their son's little drawings of 'Daddy the superhero', about the neighbours' kindness, and how they had both managed to survive these months apart, holding on to the hope of a reunion. She told him about the little things that had kept her going: the moments when she thought she saw a sign of him, the dreams she'd had, and the constant prayer that filled her every day.

"You know, the nights were the hardest," she said softly, her voice tinged with sorrow. "I tried to keep busy, but at night, the silence was overwhelming. I missed you beside me."

Arjun nodded, his throat tight. "I missed you too," he said simply.

They spoke for hours, sharing memories, recounting stories, laughing and crying over the things they had endured. Arjun told her about the bonds he'd formed with his comrades, the way they had held each other up during the darkest times. She shared how their son had started drawing pictures of their family, each one a bittersweet reminder of the life they had been forced to live apart.

As the evening deepened, Arjun finally leaned back, exhausted but at peace.

She stood to clear the empty cups, and as she did, the doorbell rang—its sharp tone breaking through the warmth of the room.

Arjun turned to her, both of them unsure of who could be at the door.

"Who could that be?" she wondered aloud, her voice tinged with surprise. "Neighbours usually don't come at this hour."

She got up from the sofa, her movements deliberate, as if steeling herself for whatever awaited on the other side of the door. Arjun watched her intently, his stare steady yet unreadable. She opened the door slowly, and there they were—two familiar figures standing in the dim light of the evening.

It was Rohit and Sameer, the latter one of Arjun's closest friends and the former whom she had met at quite a few parties. She knew them well; they, with Raghav, had often visited their home, laughing over old stories and indulging in endless cups of tea.

Her look flitted between them, searching for an explanation. Rohit avoided her eyes, his jaw tense, while Sameer's shoulders slumped as if weighed down by an invisible burden. The three of them stood in a tense, wordless moment, the unspoken stretching between them like a chasm. She couldn't understand what they were doing here at this hour of the evening, their solemn expressions so unlike the jovial friends she remembered.

Finally, breaking the heavy silence that had settled over the room, Rohit said in a voice barely above a whisper, "We're so sorry, Meera." His words trembled, as if carrying the weight of guilt too unbearable to shoulder. His eyes darted to hers for a fleeting moment before dropping to the floor again, unable to hold her gaze.

Beside him, Sameer stood motionless, his shoulders hunched, his head drooped so low it seemed as if he was trying to disappear into himself. His hands were clasped tightly together, the knuckles white, betraying the storm raging within him. He opened his mouth as if to speak but quickly shut it, his voice lost to the lump in his throat.

The words hit her like a cold gust of wind, chilling her to the bone. "Sorry? Sorry for what?"

Her confusion deepened, her mind racing to comprehend their presence, their grim demeanour. She looked at them both, hoping for clarity, but their faces revealed nothing more.

They seemed to be searching for the right words, but none came. Instead, they exchanged a glance, as if silently deciding who would speak next.

She took a step back, her heart pounding. "What... what are you sorry for?" she asked, her voice trembling. Her mind buzzed with questions, each one more alarming than the last. Were they here to deliver bad news? Had something happened to someone she knew? Why were they looking at her like that, as if they couldn't bear to meet her eyes?

She noticed for the first time that they were carrying something. She looked down instinctively, and her breath caught. They were holding a coffin. A coffin. Her entire body turned rigid, her hands gripping the edge of the doorframe for support. Her mind reeled. Why had they brought this to her house? What did it mean? Her throat tightened, and her voice, barely above a whisper, trembled as she asked, "What is this? What... what's happening?"

Sameer's voice was low, laden with sorrow. "It's Arjun," he said. "He... he didn't make it. He died while fighting at Tiger Hill. He took a bullet. It was instant."

The world seemed to tilt around her. The words didn't make sense. Her ears rang, and her vision blurred as she tried to process what he had just said. "No," she whispered, shaking her head. "No, that's not possible. Arjun is right here. He's home. He... he's sitting inside, on the sofa."

She turned and pointed toward the living room, where Arjun was sitting. He was there, wasn't he? She had felt his warmth; heard his voice. She had made him tea, and they had talked for hours. Her mind clung desperately to the memories of the evening, to the reality she had just lived.

But when Rohit and Sameer followed her look, their expressions didn't change. They looked into the house, their eyes scanning the empty sofa. "There's no one there," Sameer said softly, his voice breaking. "He... he's gone."

"No!" she cried, her voice rising in panic. "He's right there! Look! He's smiling at me. Don't you see him? He's here! He's home!" Her voice cracked as she pointed again, tears streaming down her face.

Rohit and Sameer exchanged a worried glance, their faces etched with grief and confusion.

"Maybe you need to sit down," Rohit said gently, stepping closer to her. "This is hard. We know it's hard. But you have to understand... he's gone. We've brought him home."

She shook her head violently, the tears blinding her. "No, you don't understand! He's here! He's alive! Arjun, tell them!" she pleaded, turning toward the sofa. "Tell them you're here! Tell them!"

Arjun, still sitting on the sofa, smiled at her, his expression calm and reassuring. "I'm here," he said softly, his voice steady. "But I have to go soon, Meera..."

Rohit and Sameer didn't react. They didn't turn to look at him. They couldn't hear him. They couldn't see him. And suddenly, the world around her seemed to collapse. Her knees buckled, and she sank to the floor, her sobs wracking her body.

Rohit knelt beside her, his hand on her shoulder. "We know this is hard," he said, his voice breaking. "He was a hero. He saved so many lives. But he's gone. We're here to honour him, to bring him home to you."

Her mind raced, torn between the reality they were presenting and the one she had just lived. How could he be gone when she had just held him, spoken to him, shared tea with him? Her heart ached, her chest tight with the weight of grief and confusion.

Meera stood stunned and paralysed, her hand still clutching the cap and medals they had handed her. She could feel the coldness of the fabric against her skin, and her fingers trembled as she gripped them tighter, as if trying to hold on to something that was slipping away. The medals felt like a cruel reminder of the man she had almost lost. They should have meant something to her—a testament to Arjun's bravery—but at that moment, they felt like they were trying to strip away the warmth of his presence.

She turned away from the medals, desperate for some explanation, some understanding. But when her stare fell on Arjun, sitting quietly across from her, the world seemed to tilt slightly. He wasn't smiling anymore; instead, there was a softness in his eyes—a deep, unwavering understanding that seemed to pierce her soul. She saw him clearly now, not as the soldier who had come home, but as the man she had waited for, the man she had feared she'd never see again. A wave of emotions crashed over her, and in that instant, all the years of uncertainty, of waiting, of hoping—everything—seemed to surge within her.

"You'll always have me," he said, his voice carrying a profound tenderness that reached into her heart. The weight of his words, simple yet so deep, caused her chest to tighten. His words should have been enough—should have been the closure she needed—but they weren't. She needed to know why he had left her in the dark for so long, why she had been forced to face life without him, without any answers.

And then, as if his words had unlocked something within her, she saw a light. It was faint at first, just a glimmer behind him, but it quickly grew brighter, wrapping around him like a halo. She blinked, confused, unsure of what she was seeing. The light was almost ethereal, like something out of a dream, a vision she couldn't quite grasp. She looked at Arjun, but he didn't seem to notice. His expression was serene, as if he was waiting for something, something she couldn't quite put her finger on.

Before she could make sense of it, the light intensified, and Arjun, her husband, her love—began to slowly fade, blending with the light that had surrounded him. His form seemed to dissolve into the glow, his outline softening until he was no longer there, as if he had become one with the very air around him. It was as though she was watching a part of him slip away, not in the painful, violent sense of loss, but in something peaceful, almost gentle. Meera's breath caught in her throat as she reached out, instinctively, wanting to pull him back, wanting to hold on to the man she had just gotten back. But her fingers grasped nothing but the air. She stood still, her mind unable to comprehend what was happening. The light that had enveloped him was now gone, leaving only the fading echo of his presence.

Sameer and Rohit, who had been standing quietly at the door, saw her eyes widen as if she had seen something none of them could. They exchanged a glance, unsure whether they should intervene or leave her to the moment she was having. The silence in the room was thick and oppressive, as if the air had become heavy with something neither of them could understand.

Meera didn't notice them. She couldn't—her entire focus was on the spot where Arjun had been, the space he had occupied, and where the light had devoured him. Her heart hammered in her chest, but the pain was different now. It wasn't the sharp, searing pain of loss; it was something softer, something that felt like both a release and a goodbye. She shook her head, trying to make sense of it, but nothing made sense anymore. She could no longer feel the cold floor beneath her; she didn't feel anything except the overwhelming flood of emotions that surged through her, crashing into her chest, choking her. Her mind was a whirlwind, spinning with thoughts of the past—the days when she had waited for him, the nights when she had cried herself to sleep, wondering if he would ever come back, if she would ever feel his touch again. And now, as she sat on the floor, surrounded by the silence that had once been filled with the sound of his laughter, she realised with an aching clarity that she was not alone—he was with her, in a way she couldn't fully understand, in a way she wasn't sure she was ready to accept.

Sameer and Rohit stood there, unsure of how to help, unsure if they should approach her. They had seen her go through so much, but this—this was something different. Meera's sobs filled the room, quiet at first, but then they grew louder, more desperate. She had just gotten him back, only to lose him again. And in her heart, she knew that this time, the loss was final.

***

The Heart Of A Soldier

The house was quiet that evening, the weight of tomorrow hanging heavily in the air. Meera sat with Aarav at the dining table. The boy—no, the young man—sat straight-backed, his NDA acceptance letter folded neatly next to him. Tomorrow, he would leave to start his journey as a cadet at the National Defence Academy. Meera studied him silently for a moment, her heart swelling with pride and tightening with an ache only a mother could understand.

Aarav broke the silence. "You've been quiet, Ma. Are you alright?"

Meera smiled softly, her eyes glistening. "I am alright. Just... thinking of your father."

At the mention of Arjun, Aarav's face softened. Though he had been too young to remember much about his father, the stories his mother had told him over the years had etched an image of Arjun in his mind: a brave, kind, and resolute man who had given his life fighting for his country during the Kargil War.

Meera reached across the table and placed her hand over Aarav's. "Your father did come back that night," she began, her voice steady but tinged with emotion. "The night he was brought home, I mean. He had promised he would return, and in his own way, he kept that promise. But the reality, Aarav, is that he died a warrior on Tiger Hill. He fought bravely, and his sacrifice was not in vain."

Aarav listened intently, his young face a mixture of pride and solemnity.

Meera continued, "You were so small then, barely able to understand what was happening. And now, here you are, following in his footsteps. My heart swells with pride, but I'd be lying if I said I wasn't scared. A mother always is. But I am also a soldier's wife, and I know what it means to wear this badge of honour—to serve, to protect, to sacrifice."

She paused and took a deep breath before standing up and walking to a nearby cabinet. She opened it and retrieved a small bundle of letters tied with a faded blue ribbon. Returning to the table, she placed the bundle in front of her son.

"I found these letters in your father's drawer months after he passed," she said softly. "They were written to us. One he wrote it for the day you would leave for the NDA. It's almost as if he knew, even back then, that this day would come."

Aarav's fingers trembled slightly as he untied the ribbon and found the letter addressed to him. The envelope was yellowed with time. He opened it carefully, unfolding the sheet of paper within. Meera watched as he began to read.

Dearest Aarav,

By the time you read this, you'll be a young man, ready to take on the world. I'm writing this letter with the hope that one day, you'll understand what it means to wear the uniform of our nation. If you're reading this, it means you've chosen to follow a path of honour and duty, and for that, I am endlessly proud.

Being a soldier is not just about bravery; it's about commitment, resilience, and love for your country and its people. There will be days when the burden feels heavy, but remember that you carry the hopes and dreams of millions. You are part of something larger than yourself.

I may not be there to guide you, but know that I'm with you in spirit, cheering you on every step of the way. Lean on your mother; she is the strongest person I have ever known. And never forget where you come from, for it will give you the strength to stand tall.

Be brave. Be kind. Be the man I know you're destined to be.

With all my love,

Your father

Aarav's hands shook as he lowered the letter, his throat tightening with emotion. Meera placed a hand on his shoulder, her own eyes filled with tears. "Your father believed in you, Aarav. And so do I. You have his courage, his determination. You're going to make him proud."

Aarav nodded, unable to speak. The weight of the letter, the weight of his father's words, settled in his chest, but it was not a burden. It was a mantle, a legacy he was ready to embrace.

The evening passed with conversations that flowed freely, a mix of memories, encouragement, and shared dreams. Meera made Aarav's favourite masala tea, just as she had done for Arjun so many times before. They laughed and cried, finding solace in each other's company as the night deepened.

Suddenly, the doorbell rang, breaking the quiet intimacy of the moment. Meera and Aarav exchanged a glance, both of them wondering who could be visiting at this hour.

"I'll get it," Meera said, rising from her chair. As she walked toward the door, Aarav watched her, the letter still clutched tightly in his hand. The sound of the door opening echoed through the house, followed by a sharp intake of breath from Meera.

"Who is it, Ma?" Aarav called out, his voice tinged with curiosity and concern.

Meera turned to look at him. "Aarav," she said softly, "come here."

As Aarav approached, he saw Sameer standing at the door. Dressed in his usual simple clothes, Sameer's presence instantly filled the room with warmth. Over the years, he had been much more than Arjun's comrade—he was like a brother to Meera and an uncle to Aarav, a steadfast part of their lives.

"Sameer Uncle," Aarav said, a smile breaking through the tension of the evening. "I wasn't expecting you."

Sameer stepped inside and grasped Aarav's shoulder firmly. "How could I not be here? Tomorrow marks the beginning of your journey, Aarav. I wouldn't miss this for the world."

The three of them sat together, sharing quiet conversation. The bond between them was unspoken but deeply felt, built on years of shared stories, memories, and mutual respect. After a while, Sameer reached into his pocket.

"I have something for you," Sameer said, his voice thoughtful. "It's something I've held onto for a long time. Your father gave it to me, though not directly. I found it on Tiger Hill, where we fought together. It was in a small crevice near where Arjun took his final stand."

He placed a small object in Aarav's hand. It was a pebble, smooth and dark, shaped eerily like a heart. Its natural contours were so distinct that it seemed almost sculpted by hand.

Aarav turned it over in his palm, feeling its cool surface. "A heart?" he murmured, his eyebrows furrowing.

Sameer nodded. "Your father had a habit of finding meaning in small things. When I found this, it was wedged under the edge of a rock where his gear had been. I don't know how it got there, but I knew it was meant to be kept safe. Arjun used to say, 'The heart is the strongest weapon we carry.' He believed that courage, compassion, and love are what make a soldier truly great. I think he would've wanted you to have this as a reminder."

Meera reached out, her fingers brushing the pebble in Aarav's hand. "Your father always believed in symbols," she said softly. "He would've seen this as a sign—a reminder to stay brave, but never to lose your humanity, no matter how hard the path ahead might be."

Aarav clenched the pebble tightly, his chest swelling with a mix of pride and longing. "Thank you, Sameer Uncle," he said, his voice thick with emotion.

Sameer smiled, his own eyes glinting with unshed tears. "You're ready, Aarav. You've got your father's strength, and now you carry his heart too. Wherever you go, remember what he stood for. And remember, I'll always be here for you and your mother."

That night, Aarav packed the pebble carefully into his bag, nestling it alongside his other essentials. It wasn't just a keepsake—it was a part of his father, a piece of the legacy he was about to honour.

The next morning, as Meera and Sameer stood at the gate watching Aarav leave, the young man turned back one last time. His hand instinctively brushed the pocket where he had placed the pebble, and he smiled. The road ahead was uncertain, but he carried with him a piece of his father's courage; a piece of his heart.